# Over the Edge

## Patricia H. Rushford

# Jennie McGrady Mystery Series

# Helen Bradley Mystery Series

# Over the Edge

## Patricia H. Rushford

**BETHANY HOUSE PUBLISHERS**
MINNEAPOLIS, MINNESOTA 55438

*Over the Edge*
Copyright © 1997
Patricia Rushford

Cover illustration by Sergio Giovine

Published by Bethany House Publishers
A Ministry of Bethany Fellowship, Inc.
11300 Hampshire Avenue South
Minneapolis, Minnesota 55438

Printed in the United States of America.

**Library of Congress Cataloging-in-Publication Data**

Rushford, Patricia H.
    Over the edge / by Patricia H. Rushford.
        p. — . —(Jennie McGrady mysteries ; 9)
    Summary: When his best friend is arrested for murder, Ryan teams up with his girlfriend Jennie to find the real killer.
    ISBN 1–55661–562–0 (pbk.)
    [1. Murder—Fiction.  2. Mystery and detective stories.]  I. Title.  II. Series: Rushford, Patricia H. Jennie McGrady mystery series ; 9.
PZ7.R8962Ov     997
[Fic]—dc21                            97–4713
                                          CIP
                                          AC

Dedicated to five faithful fans:
Sarah Stark,
Amanda Wilkins,
Jill Taylor,
Tiffany Naiman,
Tyler Doupe

A special thanks to my "promise ring girls"
and to my experts:
Jan Bono,
Michael Curtis,
Margo Power,
and my husband, Ron

PATRICIA RUSHFORD is an award-winning writer, speaker, and teacher who has published numerous articles and over twenty books, including *What Kids Need Most in a Mom*, *The Jack and Jill Syndrome: Healing for Broken Children*, *Have You Hugged your Tennager Today?*, and her first young adult novel, *Kristen's Choice*. She is a registered nurse and has a master's degree in counseling from Western Evangelical Seminary. She and her husband, Ron, live in Washington State and have two grown children, six grandchildren, and lots of nephews and nieces.

Pat has been reading mysteries for as long as she can remember and is delighted to be writing a series of her own. She is a member of Mystery Writers of America, Sisters in Crime, and several other writing organizations. She is also co-director of Writer's Weekend at the Beach.

# 1

"Hang on, Bernie." Jennie McGrady smiled at the St. Bernard pup who climbed into the front passenger seat. Up until then he'd been curled up on the floor in the back keeping an eye on his young master—Jennie's five-year-old brother, Nick.

"We're almost there." She slowed when she approached the gravel road leading into the quiet neighborhood north of Bay Village. Gram's house stood near the end of the street, perched on a cliff overlooking the Oregon Coast. The cool ocean air she'd hit coming over the coastal range thirty minutes before tugged at the dark strands of hair escaping her braid.

Jennie's heart tripped over itself with the prospect of spending the next two weeks here. But most of her joy—and the reason her heart had careened into overdrive—was due to the fact that she'd finally be able to hang out with Ryan Johnson. Ryan was Gram's next-door neighbor, and they had been friends for years, but early in the summer their friendship had taken on a new dimension. She'd hoped to see more of him this summer, but he'd gone fishing in Alaska. Well, he was back, and Jennie had a great vacation planned.

The subject of her dreams was at this moment walking toward her. Or maybe he was walking toward his mailbox. It didn't matter. She pulled into Gram's driveway and nearly fell flat on her face trying to get out of the car. But part of that was Bernie's fault. The dog seemed almost as excited to see Ryan as Jennie was.

Ryan closed the mailbox and waved at her, then bent to give Bernie a pat on the head. "You're early. Gram said you weren't coming until this afternoon."

Jennie's heart skidded to a stop. *Okay, Johnson, what's the deal? What kind of welcome is that? Aren't you even going to kiss me? Is it over between us? Have you found someone else?* She didn't ask any of those questions, of course, but they all tumbled around in her head when she saw the sad look in Ryan's sky-blue eyes.

His greeting didn't please Bernie either. The pup whimpered and rubbed his head against Ryan's leg.

"I'm glad you're here." His lips turned up in a half smile, then flat-lined again. He made no move to hug her as he had the last time they'd been together.

"You . . . um . . . you don't *look* glad. If I didn't know any better, I'd say you were disappointed."

Ryan shook his head, and a lock of sandy blond hair drooped onto his forehead. He brushed it back. "It's not you. I . . . I'm sorry, but something's happened and—" His Adam's apple shifted up and down as he swallowed.

He was breaking up with her—no, worse than that. Maybe something had happened to—Jennie grabbed his arm, suddenly aware of the empty driveway and the fact that Gram hadn't come out to greet them. "What? Is it Gram? J.B.?"

"No. They're fine." Ryan closed his eyes and gathered her close. "They went shopping—should be back in an hour or so."

Jennie wrapped her arms around him, resting her forehead against his chin. "Then what?" Reluctant to step out of the halfhearted embrace, Jennie tilted her head back so she could see his face. "Not your folks?"

"It's a friend of mine—Todd Kopelund." Ryan frowned and dropped his arms to his side. "He's a suspect in a murder investigation. They think he killed his girlfriend."

"Oh no. Ryan, I'm so sorry." Todd was one of Ryan's *best* friends. Lisa, Jennie's cousin and best friend, had had a crush

8

on Todd one summer a couple of years back. And no wonder. Todd had a linebacker build, eyes the color of dark chocolate, and hair that couldn't decide if it was blond or brown. "Who's—I mean, who was his girlfriend?" Jennie asked. "Do I know her?"

"Maybe. Her name was Jessica Ames. She went to a private school in Portland and was home for the summer."

"The mayor's daughter?" She did remember Jessica—talented, beautiful, and spoiled. Jennie had met her at a fundraiser of some sort that Gram had dragged her to.

"Yeah, and her folks are out for blood."

"Why was she dating Todd?" He was not only younger but definitely not on the same social level.

"He'd liked her for a long time. I never did understand what he saw in her—she was nice enough but . . ." Ryan's words trailed off. His gaze drifted back to Jennie. "He didn't do it. I know Todd, and I can't believe he'd kill anyone—especially Jessica. He loved her."

Jennie pinched her lips together partly because she didn't know what to say and partly to keep from telling him that people weren't always as they seemed. "Have you talked to Gram and J.B.?" With her grandfather being an FBI agent and Gram an ex-police officer, Jennie figured they'd have some insight on the case and might even be working on it. Gram had a thing for solving mysteries—for that matter, so did Jennie.

"Not yet. I'm not sure they even know. It happened last week while they were gone, and I haven't had much chance to talk to them."

Jennie was about to ask him for details when Mrs. Johnson opened the back door. "Ryan, telephone—it's Todd." She waved. "Hi, Jennie—welcome back. Helen called a few minutes ago—said if you got here before they did to make yourself at home. Door's unlocked."

"I'll talk to you later," Ryan called over his shoulder and jogged across the yard to his house.

Apparently feeling as rejected as Jennie did, Bernie moved up beside her and licked her hand. She absently stroked his silky coat. "I have a feeling this is going to be a long two weeks, Bern. And here I thought this vacation was going to be fun. Silly me."

When the door to the Johnson home closed, Jennie shuffled back to her Mustang and glanced into the backseat. Nick was still asleep. He'd managed to stay awake for an hour on their drive down from Portland and would probably be out for a while.

Not wanting to wake him, she pulled the key out of the ignition, gently closed the door, and opened the trunk. Might as well haul their stuff in and get settled.

Ten minutes later, while filling Bernie's water dish, Jennie heard a car door slam. She leaned over the sink to look out the kitchen window. Ryan backed his car out of the garage, whipped around, and headed down the drive, spraying gravel and raising a cloud of dust.

Her stomach knotted. Where was he going in such a hurry, and why hadn't he asked her to go with him? Not that she could have with Nick still asleep, but at least he could have asked. She had a strong hunch it had something to do with Todd.

Jennie sighed and moved away from the window, then set the dish on the back porch where Bernie waited. *Forget it, McGrady*, she told herself. *Ryan still likes you. He's just worried about his friend*. She vowed to be understanding, left the pup lapping, then went to check on Nick again.

"Hey, little buddy." Jennie pulled the seat forward and helped Nick out.

Nick scowled the way he usually did after a nap. Like a four-armed octopus, he wrapped his skinny arms and legs around her neck and waist. She carried him into the house and she settled into the rocker, nuzzling his neck. "You gonna sleep all day?"

He murmured something unintelligible against her shoulder.

Jennie smiled and kissed the top of his head. The thick black hair tickled her nose. "Bernie's waiting to play ball with you."

"Where's Gram and Papa?" Nick raised his head and let his hands drop onto his thighs.

"Shopping—bet they'll be bringing home something special for us."

Nick's navy blue eyes widened. "Like Gummi worms?"

Jennie chuckled. "Maybe. I was thinking more like crab and shrimp."

He yawned. "I'd rather have worms."

Gravel crunched as a car pulled into the driveway. Nick scampered off Jennie's lap and hit the floor running. "They're here!"

Jennie hurried after him, and the two watched Gram maneuver her classic 1955 Thunderbird convertible into the space beside Jennie's Mustang.

"Well, if it isn't two of my favorite grandchildren." J.B.'s Irish blue eyes twinkled as he stepped out of the car and spread his arms to welcome them. The way he scooped Nick up and hugged him made it seem as if he'd been a grandfather all his life instead of only a couple of months.

Jennie got her hug from J.B. and hurried around to greet Gram.

Gram wrapped her slender arms around Jennie. "It's so good to see you." Her warmth almost made up for Ryan's coolness.

"You too." Jennie gave her grandmother an extra squeeze before letting her go.

"Did your mom and dad get off all right?" Gram finger-combed her mussed-up salt-and-pepper hair.

"Yep. Which is why I'm early. Had to take them to the airport at six this morning." Jennie could almost feel her eyes brighten when she spoke. Susan and Jason McGrady were heading to Hawaii to celebrate their second marriage—to each other.

"I'm so glad they were able to resolve their differences. Did they seem happy?"

"Sickeningly so." Jennie grinned at the memory of her parents mooning over each other like newlyweds.

Gram chuckled. "Let's put these groceries away, then we'll have a nice long visit and some tea on the patio."

J.B. draped an arm around Gram's shoulder. "Why don't you two lovely ladies go on inside? The lad and I will fetch the groceries in."

"Yeah, me and Papa will do it." Nick bounced up and down waiting for J.B. to open the trunk.

Jennie followed Gram into the house. She couldn't wait to find out what, if anything, Gram knew about Jessica and Todd. Only after the groceries had been brought in and piled on the counter and the "guys" had taken Bernie for a run on the beach did Jennie have a chance to talk with Gram alone.

"How about putting these in my big fruit bowl." Gram handed Jennie a bag of various fruits and a hand-thrown bowl decorated with colorful salmon. "You'll need to wash them first."

"Sure." Jennie pulled out a large cluster of grapes, set them in a colander, and rinsed them with cold water.

"Have you seen Ryan yet?" Gram asked.

"For a minute. He left after he got a phone call from his friend Todd Kopelund. I guess the police think Todd killed Jessica Ames. Did you hear about that?"

"Yes, just a few minutes ago. We saw Annie Costello in the post office." Gram paused to stash a package of salmon in the refrigerator. "You remember her, don't you? Todd's cousin?"

Jennie frowned, trying to put a face with the name.

"She's the caterer we had when I hosted an art benefit last year."

"Oh yeah." A picture of a short, curly-headed strawberry blonde came to mind. "So what did she say?"

"She told me about Jessica, of course." Gram opened the pantry and stacked cans of tomato sauce in a tidy row next to the green beans. "Such a tragedy."

"What happened to her?" Jennie asked. "Ryan said someone killed her, but—"

"You're not planning to get involved in this, are you?" Gram interrupted.

"No. Just curious." Though Jennie was being totally honest, an opposing voice in her head practically accused her of lying.

Gram took several long seconds to respond. "Her body was found on the rocks below the Ameses' home."

Jennie shivered. Like Gram, the Ames family lived high on a cliff overlooking the ocean. It would have been about a twenty-five-foot drop. "What makes the sheriff think Todd did it?"

"I'm not sure. The authorities have been trying to ascertain whether it was an accident or if someone pushed her. Apparently Todd was the last person to see her alive."

Jennie and Gram had just finished putting away the groceries and settled into lounge chairs on the patio when the doorbell rang. Jennie, being closest, offered to get it.

"Thank goodness you're here," Mrs. Johnson sobbed once Jennie opened the door. "I need one of you to drive me into town—to the hospital."

Jennie's heart constricted remembering Ryan's hasty departure. "What's wrong?"

"Ryan's been in an accident."

# 2

"Are you sure you're not too upset to drive, Jennie?" Gram asked. "I'll be happy to take her. Or I can leave a note for J.B. and Nick and we could both go."

"No, I want to drive." Jennie blinked back an onslaught of tears. "But I'd like it if you came along."

Gram left a note on the table and hurried out to the car.

"I'm sorry to bother you about this," Mrs. Johnson said as she slid into the front seat. "It's just that with my husband out of town there's only one car, and according to the sheriff it's not exactly drivable at the moment."

"It's no bother," Gram said from the back.

Mrs. Johnson must have read the worried look on Jennie's face. "The sheriff assures me he's all right, Jennie. Just a few cuts and bruises."

Jennie swallowed back the lump in her throat and nodded. She concentrated on sticking the key into the ignition . . . backing the car around . . . and driving to the main road. During the trip to Lincoln City and the nearest hospital, Jennie half listened to the two women talk. Mostly, though, her mind was on Ryan and the accident. Maybe she was reading more into it than was actually there, but her suspicions rose like the sea at high tide and created patterns of doubt in her head. *Why now?* Mrs. Johnson told them that Ryan had gone to see Todd. Had Ryan's involvement in the case caused concern for the real killer? Was Ryan's life in danger?

*Why couldn't you stay out of it?* Jennie told the image of Ryan that invaded her brain. *Why can't you just let the police take care of things? If he's innocent, they'll let him go.*

Even as the thoughts formed, Jennie knew they weren't entirely true. Too often she had heard about cases where the wrong man or woman was arrested and sentenced and the real killer got off. When it came right down to it, she would probably do whatever it took to prove a person innocent if she believed them to be—especially a friend. Jennie sighed. She and Ryan needed to talk.

The emergency room bustled with activity—green-clad figures scurrying here and there—but Jennie's gaze focused only on the cubicle in front of her. Her stomach rebelled at the sight of blood smeared into Ryan's hair and staining parts of his blue denim shirt a dark purple. The bright lights faded Ryan's summer tan. The emergency room staff and equipment settled into a distant hum. The doctor looked up from his stitching and smiled at Mrs. Johnson when she introduced herself and Jennie.

"He's going to be fine," the doctor said. "I'll be done sewing him up in a minute."

"Should we wait outside?" Mrs. Johnson's chalky complexion suggested she'd be better off in the waiting room with Gram. Jennie grabbed a vacant chair and rolled it up behind Mrs. Johnson, suggesting she sit down. Lucky thing. Mrs. Johnson's knees buckled, and she almost ended up on the floor.

"Bless you, Jennie." She fixed her gaze on something on the other side of the room.

"Can he talk?" Jennie asked the doctor.

"Why are you asking him?" Ryan murmured. "Like he told you, I'm fine."

"You don't look fine." Jennie bit her lower lip, wishing she

15

could take back the remark and the harsh tone of her voice when she said it.

"Why are you here?"

"Because your mom asked me to drive her." *And I was afraid you'd been hurt.* Jennie decided not to say too much. Accident or not, she was beginning to resent his nasty disposition. Besides, she didn't want to let him know she still loved him in case the feeling was no longer mutual.

"Now, now, kids." The doctor straightened and winked at Jennie. "Keep that up and I may have to alter my original assessment."

"What do you mean?" Ryan asked.

"You must have hit your head harder than I thought. No guy in his right mind would pick a fight with an attractive young lady like Jennie here. Unless she's your sister. . . ."

"She's not my sister." Ryan glanced in Jennie's direction.

Jennie's face and neck warmed with a flush of embarrassment. "We're friends," she responded before he could. "At least we used to be."

"Ah . . . a disagreement. I can see we need to get you out of here, Ryan. Looks like you two need to sort things out." The doctor stood and turned to the nurse. "Put a dressing on that and clean him up, would you?"

Jennie, feeling about as useless and unwanted as a mouse, mumbled something about meeting him in the waiting area and scurried out of the room.

On the way home from the hospital, Ryan remained sullen. Even though his mother had insisted he ride in front with Jennie, he didn't say much. As she drove, Jennie reminded herself again and again that they were still friends and eventually Ryan would get over his bad mood. She vowed not to feel sorry for herself and was determined not to let anything spoil her vacation at the beach. Still, it seemed strange that Ryan would shut her out like that.

Once home they piled out of the car. Ryan managed to

mumble what sounded like an insincere thank-you and came up with a semienthusiastic "I'll see you later."

———————

Later came and went. After eating a late dinner and reading bedtime stories to Nick, Jennie made the excuse that she was tired and went up to what would be her room for the next two weeks. Of the three guest rooms in Gram's house, Jennie had always liked this one best. It was small and cozy with a daybed and a big window that faced the ocean. Jennie unpacked her bags, then flopped onto the bed to read one of the new mysteries Mom had given her for the trip.

Thinking about Mom and Dad honeymooning in Hawaii almost made her forget her disappointment over Ryan. That Mom and Dad had decided to try again had been nothing short of a miracle. Dad's homecoming had been a miracle too. Jennie couldn't remember being happier than when her parents had announced their plans to remarry.

Funny how life went. She remembered a friend once saying, *"Life is a ball, but it sometimes rolls over you."* That's how she felt now. Rolled over. Like road kill on a lonesome highway. Jennie groaned at her macabre thoughts and sat up. She didn't feel much like reading. What she wanted more than anything was to go over and drag Ryan down to the rocks where they used to spend hours talking and watching the sun go down. Only she couldn't do that. What if he said no? Besides, he'd just been in an accident.

"Okay, McGrady," she said aloud, "go by yourself. You don't need Ryan along to enjoy the sunset."

Jennie grabbed a gray sweat shirt and went downstairs. She paused to let Gram and J.B. know where she was going, then made her way down the familiar path and out onto the rocks. Someone was already sitting there. Jennie thought about leaving.

"Don't go." Ryan turned toward her. "I was hoping you'd come."

*Why, so you could break up with me face-to-face?* That's what she felt like saying. What she actually said was, "You were?"

"Yeah. I need to ask you a favor."

Jennie teetered on the narrow rock ledge, then picked her way around the chasm that separated them. When she reached his side, he grabbed her hand and pulled her down beside him.

"So what's the favor?" Jennie looked at the hand that still held hers. She didn't want to look at his face or into his eyes, didn't want to think about what might be written there.

"In a minute. First, I want to tell you I'm sorry about the way I acted today. I know there's no excuse, but . . ." He shook his head. "Let's just say it's been a rotten day all around. It started with Todd telling me he was leaving town."

"That doesn't sound like a very smart move." She looked at him then, watching his profile as he spoke into the wind.

"I told him that." Ryan glanced at her, then turned back toward the ocean.

"Did he leave?" Jennie tried to concentrate on their conversation and not on the emotions churning around inside her like the boiling water in the deep crevices below.

"Not exactly. He got as far as Whale Cove when the sheriff arrested him."

"That must mean they have a case against him."

Ryan nodded. "So they say. I haven't been able to find out anything." He shifted his gaze back to Jennie. This time he didn't turn away.

Jennie's heart stopped, and she couldn't breathe.

Ryan reached out to cup her chin. "I've missed you."

"I . . ." The words melted as Ryan's lips connected with hers.

It was a short kiss, but definitely a kiss, and Jennie rated it a ten. Her heart started again, racing faster than a sandpiper in the surf. She wanted a repeat performance, but Ryan had turned away and was watching the lavender and pink sky.

"I'd like to borrow your car."

Jennie pulled her hand free of his grasp. "You really are a piece of work, Johnson. You act like I don't exist, then all of a sudden you're apologizing and . . ." She scrambled to her feet.

"Wait a minute." Ryan jumped up and blocked her path. "What did I do?"

"As if you didn't know." She gave him a shove. Ryan slipped on the rock and started to fall backward, waving his arms in the air.

Jennie grabbed his hand and yanked him toward her. She landed on her rear and slid down the incline, grabbing at the craggy rock face. Her foot caught in a crevice, jerking her to a stop.

"What were you trying to do, kill me?" Ryan caught himself and reached for her hand, hauling her up and into his arms.

"I'm sorry," Jennie gasped. Beneath her ear, his chest seemed to be beating as wildly as hers. "I thought you were using me and . . ."

Ryan leaned back. "What are you talking about?"

*Okay, McGrady, think for once before you speak. Maybe you're wrong about Ryan making up with you just so he can borrow your car.* She had to know.

"Ryan, do you still like me?"

"Of course I do. Why would you ask a stupid question like that?"

"Maybe I'm reading you wrong here, but the way you were acting when I arrived this morning and again at the hospital, I had the distinct impression you were planning on breaking up with me."

His shoulders slumped. He let go of her and dropped

down to the rock. "It's not you, Jennie. I still feel the same way about you as I did before. I thought you knew that. It's this whole thing with Todd. I've been so wrapped up in that, I haven't been able to think straight. Which is why I ended up ramming the car into the back of a truck."

Jennie felt like a jerk. She'd been so caught up in her own feelings she hadn't taken the time to really think about what Ryan must be going through. "Ryan, I'm so sorry." She laced her fingers through his. "About the car. I can't let you drive it. The insurance only covers Mom and me right now. Not that I don't trust you, it's just that Mom would probably ground me for the rest of my life if I let anyone else drive it."

"It's okay. I can probably find someone else—"

Jennie thumped his arm. "I wasn't finished. I was going to say that I can't let you drive the car, but I'll drive you wherever you need to go."

Ryan draped an arm around her shoulder. "Thanks, Jennie, but I can't let you do that."

"Why? Are you planning on going places you shouldn't?"

"No . . . it's just that—"

"You want to find out what really happened to Jessica, right?"

He nodded. "I guess maybe I do. I know it sounds stupid. Like what can I do?"

"*We.* I'm not sure we can do anything. But I'm getting pretty good at this sort of thing."

"I know, but this is different. Somebody killed a girl our age. I wouldn't want anything to happen to you."

"I don't want anything to happen to you, either, but if we work together we can protect each other. I don't know the details, but if you really believe Todd is innocent, then I'll do whatever I can to help you prove it."

Ryan squeezed her hand and pulled her closer. "You make it sound so easy. Maybe I should have more faith. I try, it's just that when the sheriff actually arrested Todd today, I got this hopeless feeling. Like it was all over."

Jennie didn't answer. She knew the feeling all too well. She squeezed his hand and leaned against him. Shoulder to shoulder they sat and watched the brilliant red sun sink into the sea. While they waited for the moon, they talked about family and fishing, and Jennie brought Ryan up-to-date on her dad's homecoming.

Ryan had been in Alaska most of the summer working on a commercial fishing boat. He was excited to be home but depressed at the thought of having to go back to school soon. Now with the murder and his best friend in jail, he felt at odds.

"I hate to say it, Jennie, but we'd better go back." Ryan stood and gave Jennie a hand up.

"I'm glad I came out here tonight."

"Me too."

They scrambled over the familiar rocks and headed into the woods. Neither had remembered a flashlight, but they didn't need one—they'd walked the same path a hundred times before. When they reached Gram's yard, Ryan stopped. "We should talk about tomorrow."

"Sure. What about it?"

"I need you to drive me to the courthouse in the morning. Todd's being arraigned at nine-thirty. I want to talk to Greg and Annie about getting enough money together for bail."

"Who's Greg?"

"Todd's brother."

"Did I miss something? Why would you talk to his cousin and his brother about bail—what about his parents?"

"They're dead. His mom died of cancer when he was little. He lost his dad in a logging accident several years back. Greg sort of took over raising Todd."

"That's so sad."

"Yeah. They've had a rough time. Anyway, none of them

make much money. I thought if we went together maybe we could come up with enough."

"Do you really think they'll let him out?" Jennie doubted it—not on a murder charge.

"Maybe. He's never been in trouble before—at least not that I know of."

"I need to talk to Gram and make sure she can take care of Nick."

"There's one more thing I want to do. It won't be very pleasant, but maybe we'll find something." Ryan chewed on his lower lip.

"What's that?"

"Visit the scene of the crime."

# 3

Jennie woke from a fitful sleep the next morning. She kept imagining Jessica Ames falling to her death on the jagged rocks below her home. Sometimes the victim's face was Jessica's—sometimes it was Jennie's. Try as she might, she couldn't stop the images from hurling themselves into her mind.

She kept remembering how she'd pushed Ryan and almost lost him. What if Ryan had fallen into the fierce, pounding surf? Would she be facing murder charges?

At eight-fifteen, Jennie gave up the notion of sleep and crawled out of bed. A shower revived her, and at eight-forty-five she headed downstairs.

"Ryan called while you were in the shower. Wanted to make sure you were up." Gram set half a grapefruit and a bowl of oatmeal on the table.

"Where are J.B. and Nick?" Jennie settled into a chair, then poured a glass of orange juice.

Gram chuckled. "Off doing guy stuff. J.B. took him down to the dock to watch the fishing boats. He said something about teaching the 'lad' how to fish."

"That's neat." Jennie had told Gram and J.B. of her plans to meet with Ryan the night before, and they'd agreed to watch Nick. "J.B.'s really good at being a grandfather. Nick sure loves him."

"The feeling's mutual. J.B.'s never been around children much, so he's having the time of his life." Gram poured a cup of hot water from the teapot and sat down beside Jennie. "I'm glad to see you and Ryan are speaking again."

Jennie shrugged. "Guess he has a hard time focusing on more than one thing at once. I thought he didn't like me, but he's just too worried about Todd to notice much else."

"And now?"

"He says nothing has changed between us." Jennie sighed. "He's hoping I'll help him find evidence to prove Todd didn't kill Jessica."

"You'll be seeing Todd today, is that right?"

"Uh-huh."

"I'll be anxious to hear what you think after you talk to him."

Jennie set her spoon down. "Is there something you're not telling me?" Gram had that knowing look in her eyes.

"No, it's just a feeling I have—and this." Gram handed her a folded newspaper and pointed to the headline. *Suspect Arrested in Ames Murder.* Jennie scanned the article, her heart sinking. It didn't look good for Todd. According to an interview with Mayor Ames, Todd had been the last person to see Jessica alive. Todd claimed he was innocent and that he had dropped Jessica off around ten and gone home. But Mrs. Ames says she saw them sitting by the stone wall much later than that. And Mayor Ames claims he saw Todd drive away just as he was coming home at midnight. Jennie almost cried when she read the quote from the mayor: *"I went to her room to say good-night. Her light was on, but she wasn't there, so I asked Mari if she'd seen her. Mari said to look outside. Jessica loved to sit in the gazebo or on the wall at night. That's when I found her."*

Jennie set the paper on the table, her breath swishing out. "You think Todd's guilty, don't you?"

Gram took a sip of her tea before answering. "At this

point I don't know enough to speculate."

Jennie twisted her braid around her hand. "I have a question for you. Mayor Ames found Jessica late at night, right?"

"According to the reports, yes."

"Hmm."

"What are you thinking?" Gram set her cup down and leaned forward.

"That the mayor might have killed her."

"Really. How do you come up with that?"

Jennie chewed on her lower lip. "Why would he have looked over the edge? It seems strange to me. You'd think he'd search the house and grounds first. It was like he knew where to look."

Gram nodded. "Perhaps, but he may have paused to look at the ocean and happened to see her."

"Yeah—but it was dark. How could he have seen anything twenty some feet below him?"

"Flood lights, Jennie. They light up the area at night. I would imagine he turned them on before he went to look for her."

"Oh." Embarrassed, Jennie picked up the paper again.

"It was valid question," Gram said, encouraging her like always. "And I'm sure the investigating officers asked the same thing."

Jennie glanced over the incriminating article. "It looks bad for Todd, doesn't it?"

"Yes, it does. Forrest and Mari Ames are reputable people. I doubt they'd lie about something like this."

"Looks like Ryan and I have our work cut out for us." Jennie shifted her gaze to Gram, expecting the usual word of caution—wishing in a way Gram would tell her to forget about it. "Aren't you going to warn me to be careful?"

"Do I need to?"

"No. I won't take any unnecessary chances, and I'll let you know what I'm doing and call you or the sheriff if I find anything that might be important to the case."

"Well, then you'd better get a move on." She glanced at her watch. "Ryan should be here any minute."

"After we talk to Todd, Ryan wants to go over to where Jessica's body was found. Do you think that's a good idea?"

"Sounds as if you're not very excited about it." Gram spread a dab of cream cheese on a cinnamon-raisin bagel.

"It seems kind of gruesome. Anyway, the sheriff will have taken away any evidence, so we won't be able to see anything."

"Sometimes being there helps to put yourself in the victim's place."

Jennie shuddered. "I've been doing that all night."

"Are you feeling all right, dear? You don't seem your usual perky self."

Jennie pushed her empty dish toward the center of the table. She wasn't feeling all that great. Maybe it was the dream. All morning she'd had an uneasy feeling and couldn't seem to shake it. As much as she wanted to learn about the case, she found herself growing more and more reluctant. The article hadn't helped matters. "I'm okay, I guess. I'm just not sure I'm ready to go to this hearing. What I really want to do is find a secluded beach and read a novel." She scrunched up her nose. "I know this sounds weird coming from me, but I'm not sure I want to get involved."

"Why don't you call Ryan and tell him you can't go? You can lie around and read—take a nice warm bubble bath and a nap—"

The doorbell rang, and Ryan let himself in.

"Sounds good, Gram," Jennie said, "but Ryan needs my car. Besides, I promised."

"Promised what?" Ryan sauntered in, whipped a chair around, and straddled it, resting his arms on the chair back.

"That I'd make sure you stayed out of trouble." Jennie

picked up her dishes and set them in the sink and began rinsing them.

"Leave those, Jennie. You two run along."

After a hasty good-bye, Jennie and Ryan headed for the courthouse.

"I appreciate you driving me." Ryan clasped his hands in front of him, resting them on his knees. "I hate being without wheels. The mechanic says it'll be another week before I can get the car back."

"No problem. I'll be around."

Ryan heaved a sigh, flashed her a nervous grin, then fixed his gaze on the car in front of them.

Jennie wanted to say something intelligent or encouraging, but the right words evaded her. She couldn't very well tell Ryan everything would be okay when she had no idea whether it would or not. "So, how's your head?"

He gave her a blank look. "My head?"

"Yeah, you were in an accident yesterday, remember?"

He touched the white square dressing on his forehead. "Oh, um—fine. It hardly hurts at all." Ryan was spaced-out again, no doubt thinking of Todd.

Fortunately the ride to the courthouse lasted only a few minutes. The gravel crunched as Jennie pulled into the unpaved lot and parked beside a dark green Lexus.

"The mayor's here." Ryan thumped the roof of her car. "I was afraid he'd show up."

Ryan's uneasiness filtered through to her. "I take it that's not good."

"If Ames has his way, Todd will be put away for life." Ryan headed for the courthouse, and Jennie hurried to catch up with him.

According to the date etched into a beige stone rock above the entry, the courthouse had been built in 1910. Their footsteps echoed on the marble floor as they entered.

"Ryan!" Annie hurried toward them. "I'm glad you

came. Todd needs all the support he can get." She glanced at Jennie and smiled. "I should know you—don't tell me." Her green eyes brightened in recognition. "You're Helen's granddaughter, Jennie."

"Right." Jennie slid her hand along the thin strap of her small handbag.

"I'm Todd's cousin, Annie. It's good to see you again."

"You too," Jennie replied.

"Did you get my message?" Ryan asked. "About going together on the bail?"

Annie nodded. "Greg told me. I have no idea what it will be. A lot, I expect—if the judge will even let him out. He's getting a lot of pressure from the mayor and the press. Greg isn't sure he wants to put up bail even if the judge sets it."

"Why not? We can't just leave Todd in jail. He didn't do it."

"Money's tight for him, Ryan—for me too." She pinched her lips together, letting her gaze drop to the floor. "Besides, we really don't know for sure that he's innocent."

"That's crazy." Ryan shoved his hands into his pockets and frowned. "You know Todd would never hurt anyone—especially Jessica."

Annie glanced at the oversized watch on her thin wrist. "We should go inside," she said, then added, "Greg's late—he should have been here by now."

Before Ryan could respond, the object of their discussion walked in. Wearing faded jeans and a plaid flannel shirt, Greg looked like he'd just come off his boat—which he probably had. Greg Kopelund was about Ryan's height and nearly twice as broad across the chest and shoulders. His short ash brown hair, mussed by the wind, settled neatly into place when he ran a hand through it. From the stern look on his face, the courthouse was the last place Greg wanted to be. He paused to greet Ryan and Jennie, then followed Annie into the courtroom.

At least twenty people were already seated on the scarred old benches. Half a dozen spectators, probably reporters, judging by the steno pads, sat in the back row. Annie and Greg went to the front and eased into the second row behind the defense table. Mayor Ames and his wife, Mari, sat opposite them on the side of the prosecution. Jennie's heart lurched when she saw them. How awful for them to have lost a daughter, then face the person thought to have done it. Mari Ames turned and caught Jennie watching her. For a moment neither looked away.

Jennie broke eye contact when she felt the pressure of Ryan's hand on her back, guiding her into a bench seat three rows behind Annie and Greg. For some inexplicable reason, Jennie felt like a traitor. She should be sitting on the other side—with Jessica's parents. Mari Ames' haunting look made Jennie's heart ache all the more.

"Todd's got a court-appointed lawyer," Ryan whispered. "I hope she's good." He nodded toward the woman seated at a table in front of the railing. The attorney pulled a file folder out of her open briefcase, then glanced over at the prosecuting attorney. Her smile told Jennie they may be on opposite sides in the courtroom, but not on the outside.

"I wonder who appointed her," Ryan added when he saw the interchange between the two. A door to the right near the judge's desk opened, and a deputy ushered Todd in. Todd looked smaller than his six feet, probably because of the slump of his shoulders and the way his head drooped. His chocolate brown gaze settled on Ryan, then shifted briefly to Jennie. He turned around and sat down beside his attorney. Gram had often said you could read a person's heart by looking into their eyes. In Todd's she'd read neither guilt nor innocence. One thing was for sure, though. Todd Kopelund was one frightened and unhappy young man. She just wished she could share Ryan's conviction.

"All rise," a bailiff ordered in preparation for the judge's entrance.

A man Jennie recognized as Charlie Crookston hurried in, his robe billowing around his small frame. In addition to being a judge, Charlie ran an ice cream parlor on main street. Jennie and Gram had spent many afternoons there sipping lattés and eating pistachio ice cream cones. In his shop, Charlie would always stop to chat with her and Gram. Today, however, he was all business. Grim faced, he mounted the stairs behind the bench and gave Todd a glare that could melt steel at fifty paces. Charlie had a reputation for being tough on crime. From where Jennie sat, things did not look good for Ryan's friend.

"Lincoln County Court is now in session, the honorable Charles Crookston presiding."

The judge slammed the gavel on the desk to make it legal.

Thirty minutes later it was over. Todd pleaded innocent and was bound over for trial. The court date had been set for two weeks from the day, and Todd would be held without bail. The prosecuting attorney had presented a strong case against setting bail, citing the fact that Todd had tried to flee the day before. Todd's court-appointed attorney had argued in Todd's defense, citing that the evidence collected so far was circumstantial and that Todd had never had so much as a traffic citation. The judge disagreed.

Jennie didn't say so, but had she been the judge, she'd have made the same decision. Something she didn't dare tell Ryan.

"Can you believe those guys?" Ryan squeezed into the passenger seat of her Mustang and slammed the door. "I mean, it's like they've got him tried and convicted already." He shook his head. "And that lawyer—bet anything the mayor paid her to go along with the prosecution."

Jennie cleared her throat. "I doubt that, Ryan. You have

to admit Todd brought it on himself. He shouldn't have tried to leave town."

"He was scared."

Wanting to change the subject, Jennie asked, "Are you hungry?"

"Not really, but I guess we'd better eat. Let's get something at the Burger Hut and take it to the beach. We have to plan our next move."

Jennie had no idea what the next move would be. All she could think about was the condemning newspaper article she'd read that morning and the pain-filled faces of the murdered girl's parents at the arraignment. But the most vivid in her mind was the mayor's outburst when Todd was leaving the courtroom. Mayor Ames had stood up and pointed an accusing finger at Todd and yelled, "He killed her! That animal killed my little girl!"

# 4

"I never thought I'd say this, Gram, but I'm so glad Ryan decided to go home and rest. I can hardly stand to be around him." Jennie dropped onto the couch and tipped her head back against the cushions. After lunch Ryan had complained of a headache and opted to take a nap before heading over to the jail to see Todd and then visiting the crime scene.

Gram looked up from her computer. After retiring from police work, Gram had turned to writing. "Sounds serious. What's the trouble?"

"He's too intense, for one thing. He's too close to Todd to be objective," Jennie groaned. "I'm afraid to say anything because I might upset him. He's totally freaked out that Judge Crookston wouldn't let Todd out on bail."

"I take it the hearing didn't go well then."

"You could say that."

Gram rolled her chair back from the desk and picked up her mug. "Why don't you come into the kitchen? We can talk over tea."

Tea was Gram's answer to just about everything. Jennie dutifully followed her grandmother into the brightly lit room, selecting a chair bathed in sunshine. Gram placed two cups in the microwave, then set cranberry scones and butter on the table and waited for the water to heat.

When the water was ready, Gram dunked a tea bag in her

cup. "Now tell me what happened at the hearing."

Jennie related the essentials. "I guess the defense has enough evidence to bring the case to trial and to keep Todd in jail." Jennie sipped at her peppermint tea. The quiet scent calmed her jangled nerves. "Ryan won't accept the fact that Todd might have done it."

"Do you think he did?"

Jennie set her cup on the table. "To be honest, I don't know what to think. Mr. and Mrs. Ames were so devastated. I felt like . . . like a traitor."

"I'm not sure I understand."

"Me either. I felt like I was rooting for the wrong guy just by sitting on the same side of the room as Todd. What if he did it, like the mayor says? I'm not sure I want to be on Todd's side—but I don't want Ryan to be mad at me either."

"Why do you have to be on anyone's side? If it bothers you so much, don't get involved."

"It's not that easy. I can't stop thinking about Jessica, and I want to know for sure who killed her."

"That's a tall order." Gram rubbed her finger over the ridges of her cup. "What do you plan to do?"

"Nothing right now." After a few seconds Jennie stood up. "I'm going down to the rocks to read—unless you need me to help you with something."

"No, you go ahead. I have to get back to work. I'm hoping to finish my article before J.B. and Nick get back."

"They're still fishing?"

Gram smiled. "Not exactly. They've gone to the aquarium in Newport to see the whale."

"Keiko? I should have gone with them. I haven't seen him yet." The famous whale from the *Free Willy* movie had been brought to Oregon from Mexico, and Jennie had planned to ask Ryan if he'd go to the aquarium with her. Another disappointment. Until this business with Todd and Jessica was over, she doubted Ryan would want to do anything.

"Perhaps you and I will go. I'm certain J.B. and Nick would love to visit Keiko again."

Jennie headed to her room to retrieve a book, then slipped out the front door and took the familiar path to the rocks. Once there she settled into a crevice resembling a reclining chair and started reading. Two pages later Jennie had no idea what she'd read. Her mind kept drifting back to Jessica.

Jennie was sitting only about half a mile from where it happened. She could climb over the rocks and get to the Ameses' place within ten minutes. Almost of their own volition, her hands pressed against the rocks and her knees bent. She jumped to her feet, stuffed her book in her back pocket, and scrambled over the rough rock formations created by some ancient volcano. Only hours ago, she'd been squeamish about visiting the scene of the crime—now she couldn't wait to get there.

It took longer than she expected, but that was because of the tricky places where she had to wait for water to recede before moving on. It wasn't until she reached the estate—or rather the rocks in front of the estate—that she began to question the wisdom of her venture.

High above her, at the top of a sheer cliff, stood a gray stone wall. Not far below lay the surging and powerful Pacific Ocean. Jessica had fallen over the cliff and landed somewhere near where she was standing. Jennie swallowed back the catch in her throat. It seemed odd being there. Like she was trespassing or something. Not that Jennie was superstitious or even believed in ghosts, but she simply couldn't get over the feeling that she needed to somehow be where Jessica had been and see the people Jessica had seen before her death. Following the footsteps of a dead girl might prove difficult—maybe even deadly.

Definitely eerie. Maybe coming here had been a mistake. "You should have thought of that sooner," she muttered to herself. Jennie shivered, wishing she'd thought to bring a jacket or sweat shirt. The wind had picked up and now blew through her thin cotton T-shirt. Clouds were gathering to the west. She'd have to head back soon.

Despite the cold, she sat on the outcropping of rocks and gazed out over the ocean. After a few minutes of not moving except to tip her head to watch the screeching sea gulls, an odd sensation crept up her spine. Was she being watched? She twisted around, her gaze traveling the length of the stone wall, but saw no one. When she turned back, she caught sight of something shiny tucked into one of the many crevices on the rock face just beneath her. A piece of jewelry? Chances are it was just one of those aluminum rings from a pop can, but she had to find out.

Jennie scooted forward but couldn't reach it without falling headfirst into the water. Maybe if she got on her stomach she could hook her toes over a ridge and stretch out. She did and managed to snare the object. It was a ring all right, but not aluminum. The letters inscribed in the dainty gold band read *True Love Waits*. Jennie had seen rings like it before. Several girls in her youth group at church had gotten them as a symbol of their vow to remain sexually pure until marriage. Had it been Jessica's? If so, why wasn't it on Jessica's hand rather than on the rocks?

Jennie placed the ring on her finger for safe keeping and glanced up at the gray wall, wishing God would give her some answers. Water crashed against the rocks and splashed into the crevice where she'd found the ring. Panic clawed at Jennie's stomach.

*The tide.*

How could she have been so stupid? She hadn't bothered to check the tide schedule, and now it was too late. The way she'd come and the only way out was now a swollen, churning chasm of ocean and seaweed. As she searched the cliff for possible footholds, another wave hit, swirling around her feet and drenching her shoes and ankles.

"Help!" she screamed. With any luck someone might be in the Ameses' yard and could toss her a rope. What started out as a second cry for help ended in a scream as another wave hit. It crashed onto the rock, sending a wall of water over her. Jennie fell to her knees and clawed at the rock as her body slid downward.

# 5

The wave dissipated, leaving Jennie's legs dangling over the edge of the precipice. She crawled arm over arm back to where she'd been standing. Another wave like that and she'd end up as fish food. The chilling salt water clung to her clothes and dripped from her hair into her eyes.

"Come on, McGrady, move," Jennie grunted as she pulled herself up another few inches, nearly cheering when her knee finally connected with the ledge.

"Hey! What are you doing down there?"

Jennie was almost afraid to look up—afraid the voice calling down to her was only a figment of her overactive imagination.

"Hey, you! Do you need some help?"

Jennie brushed aside her dripping bangs and tipped her head back. A young boy about fourteen peered over the wall.

Jennie waved and yelled, "I'm trapped down here. Can you get a rope?"

"Hang on—be right back!"

"Hurry!" Jennie glanced back at the ocean and scrambled to her feet, grasping the finger-thin branch of a shrub that jutted out from the rock just inches above her head. Another wave smashed against her, this time reaching to her waist. When she looked up, the boy was gone.

Minutes later he returned with a yellow nylon rope and a

friend. Issuing orders for her to slip her foot into the loop at the end, they lowered it. Jennie grabbed on and swung away from the sheer rock face, using her free foot to keep from slamming into the cliff.

"Okay, hold on and we'll pull you up."

Jennie did, praying the rope wouldn't fray as it strained against the rock and concrete.

Inch by inch they hauled her up. When she reached the top of the stone wall, she hooked an arm over it and anchored herself. Moments later she sat looking back at where she'd been. The rocks below disappeared under another crashing wave. Jennie turned away and gasped out a thank-you to her rescuers.

"No problem."

"I was afraid no one would hear me," Jennie said breathlessly.

"Are you kidding?" The boy brushed back his straight brown hair and slapped on a silver-and-blue baseball cap with a logo that read *Dallas Cowboys*. "Me and Don could hear you clear from my room." He pointed toward the three-story house. "Who are you, anyway?"

"Jennie McGrady." Jennie wrapped her arms around herself and bit her lip. The wind off the ocean was quickly turning her into an ice cube.

"Oh yeah, I remember seeing you around. You're Ryan Johnson's girlfriend."

"Used to be. These days I'm not so sure. You must be Jessica's brother."

"Yep. I'm Micky."

"How'd you get down there?" the other boy asked.

"I was exploring. My grandmother lives around on the other side of the inlet. Ah . . ." She turned to Micky. "Do you think I could borrow a dry shirt or something? I'm freezing."

"Sure." Micky grinned. "Come up to the house. You could probably fit into my sister's clothes. She was about your size." His eyes clouded, and he glanced away.

Jennie followed the boys through the back entrance and large kitchen, then up a flight of stairs.

"My sister's room is in there." Micky stopped at a closed door in the middle of the long hallway and glanced up at her. "There's lots of clothes and stuff in her closet."

"Dork." Don elbowed his friend. "She probably wants a hot shower first." He raised his eyebrows and looked at her, not quite meeting her eyes, then stuffed his hands in the pockets of his baggy shorts. "You'll have to excuse Micky—he's not used to rescuing pretty girls."

Micky scowled. "Yeah, like *you* are." He turned to Jennie and said, "There's a bathroom back there." Micky pointed to the left side of the room. "It's got towels and everything."

"Thanks. Um, listen, guys. You were great back there . . . you saved my life. I wish there were something—"

"Hey, no problem." Don grinned. The boys started to go, looking like a set of twins from behind. Don turned back around. "We'll be in the kitchen making some hot chocolate. That'll warm you up."

Micky whacked him in the arm. "Get real, toad-head."

"What?"

Jennie closed the door and tried to ignore the odd sensation creeping up her spine. She hurried into the bathroom and stripped out of the still-dripping shorts and T-shirt, discarding her now saturated mystery novel. After waiting for the water to warm, she ducked under the shower head and didn't emerge for fifteen minutes.

Feeling ten times better, Jennie stepped into Jessica's bedroom. The large, bright room had windows overlooking the beach. The walls and carpet were all off-white. The only color came from pastel peach, mint green, and soft pink pillows and large watercolor paintings of seashells and beach scenes in the same colors. Flouncy sheer curtains hung on the windows. Jessica's full-size bed had an antique brass frame. The bed, covered with an ivory down comforter, faced the windows and offered a spectacular view—a view of the very place where her body had been found.

Jennie shivered, wrapped her arms around herself, and moved away from the window.

A historical novel lay on the nightstand. Jennie reached for it, then snatched her hand back. *You shouldn't be snooping, McGrady.* Pulling the towel more tightly around her, she entered the walk-in closet and grabbed an oversized pink shirt and a pair of denim shorts from the nearest shelf. When she did, a book dropped to the floor. Jennie stooped to pick it up. It was a small booklet on overcoming addictions to gambling. Strange. She turned to the page marked by a brochure from the Soaring Eagle Casino at Siletz Bay. On the page were ten questions on how to tell if you're addicted to gambling.

"Whoa," Jennie mumbled aloud. "Whoever took this test definitely has a problem." Jessica? Or maybe she was taking the test for someone else—like Todd or one of her parents? Jennie set the book on the shelf and tucked the information away. Later she'd ask Ryan if either Todd or Jessica or someone else she'd known had a gambling problem.

After finding the appropriate underclothes, Jennie got dressed. Micky had been right; Jessica and she were close to the same size. The shorts, a size eight, fit perfectly. Jennie gathered up her damp clothes, wrapped them in a towel, and headed for the door—then stopped. *What are you thinking? You're in Jessica's room. What better way to find out more about her?* She argued with herself for a moment, then decided maybe it wouldn't hurt to look around.

Jennie set her bundle of clothes, towels, and shoes in a white wicker chair and moved back into the center of the room. She stood there awhile—listening, waiting—getting a feel for Jessica's personal space. She again had the oddest sensation of being watched. Yet there was no one in the room or at the windows. Jennie's heart skittered into high gear.

Unsettled and frightened as she felt, Jennie forced herself to walk over to a dresser to look at the various photos. One of Jessica and Todd standing in front of a boat. Another, a family portrait of the Ames family with a background of trees. A candid snapshot of Micky and his friend making faces at the camera.

Still another showed Jessica and a second girl in front of a tall and elaborate sand castle. Jennie remembered seeing her before as well, but couldn't think where. She turned the photo over, and a brief note read, *Camilla and me at Cannon Beach.* Jennie studied the girl's features—a small, pixielike face framed by straw-colored short hair.

Jennie picked up an eight-by-ten portrait of Jessica and focused on the flawless face smiling back at her. "I wish I'd known you better. Did you love Todd? Was it your ring I found? How did the ring end up on the rocks? How did you end up on the rocks?"

Jennie heard a noise behind her and spun around. The door to Jessica's room opened.

Mrs. Ames stepped in and fastened her startled gaze on Jennie. She dropped the vase and flowers she'd been holding and screamed. Then fainted.

41

# 6

Half an hour later, Jennie, the boys, and Mrs. Ames sat in the family room off the kitchen. Jennie took a sip of hot chocolate while she listened to Micky explain why she had been in Jessica's room.

"I understand that, Micky. Saving Jennie's life was admirable—an act of heroism." Mrs. Ames folded and refolded the wet washcloth Jennie had placed on her forehead after she'd fainted. "But why couldn't you have told me she was here?" She heaved a shuddering sigh. "Jennie, I do hope you'll forgive me. I . . . when I saw you standing there I thought . . . well . . . with you wearing Jessica's clothing and all, I thought you were her."

"I'm sorry, Mrs. Ames," Jennie said for the umpteenth time. "I didn't mean to frighten you." Jennie hadn't meant to stay so long either. Gram would be worried. And Ryan would be—what? Worried? Angry? She'd told him she'd pick him up fifteen minutes ago. "Do you think I could use your phone? I need to call my grandmother."

Mrs. Ames nodded and directed Jennie to the ivory phone on the wall near the pantry in the kitchen.

Gram thanked God that Jennie had survived, then scolded her for not being more careful of the tide. "Do you need me to come pick you up?" she asked.

"Would you?" Jennie glanced down at her clothes. "And

maybe you could bring me clean jeans and a shirt and underwear. I'm wearing Jessica's stuff right now."

Micky and Don left to go skateboarding right after Jennie hung up. Saying good-bye, she thanked them again. While she waited for Gram, Jennie sat on the sofa, wishing she could think of something comforting to say to Mrs. Ames.

All Jennie could think of was to offer another apology.

Mrs. Ames patted Jennie's hand. "It's all right. Please don't give it another thought. It's just that when someone you love dies . . . I guess everything reminds you of them."

Jennie nodded. "Mrs. Ames, can I ask you something?"

"About Jessica?"

"Yeah—but if it will upset you too much . . ."

Mrs. Ames closed her eyes and opened them as if bracing herself for a painful procedure. "What would you like to know?"

"When I got the clothes out of her closet I found a book—about gambling addiction."

"Gambling? I don't understand. Why would she have a book like that?"

"I was hoping you could tell me."

"I have no idea."

"Was Jessica into gambling?" Jennie persisted.

"Absolutely not." Mrs. Ames fumbled with her damp tissue, picking off little pieces and rolling them into balls. "She was too young, of course, but even if she'd been of age, Jessica was against gambling. We all are. She and her father and I have lobbied against all the casinos in Oregon. The only reason she'd have a book like that would be if she were studying the subject or trying to help someone else. Jessica was like that—always helping others."

"That thought crossed my mind. Any idea who she might have wanted to help?"

"Todd maybe. Or Todd's brother. Greg has been known to frequent the casinos and the bars."

Jennie wondered if the gambling thing was somehow connected to Jessica's death. A definite possibility and one she intended to pursue. First, though, she needed to ask about the ring. Jennie pulled it from her pocket and showed it to Mrs. Ames. "Do you recognize this?"

Mari Ames' already pale skin turned even whiter. "It's Jessica's. Todd gave it to her on her birthday not quite a year ago. She never took it off. How. . . ?"

"I found it down on the rocks."

Jennie had other questions but decided not to ask them. Mrs. Ames seemed to be preoccupied with something. Her eyes had glazed over, and she stared out at the green expanse of lawn.

Jennie's gaze took the same path—the one trailing through the grass to the white gazebo and hanging baskets of ferns and flowers. A perfect spot to bring friends and talk—Jessica would have done that. Somehow Jennie knew without asking that Todd had sat on the bench there with Jessica, laughing, holding hands. It might have been where he gave her the ring.

A huge question draped itself across Jennie's mind. Why had Jessica taken the ring off? Had she been about to break up with Todd?

The doorbell rang, bringing them both back to the present. Jennie absently slipped the ring back on her finger. "I'll get it," she offered. "It's probably Gram."

It was. Jennie changed clothes in the large main bathroom. It felt good to be in her own clothing. Thinking about Jessica had left her tired and frustrated. When she'd finished dressing and brushing her hair back into a ponytail, she made her way down the wide hall to the high-ceiling living room where Gram and Mrs. Ames were deep in conversation. The room looked like an art gallery featuring dozens of paintings and sculptures.

Mrs. Ames held a fresh tissue in her hand. "I do hope you'll be there, Helen. I've invited three of my favorite local artists. We'll be showing their work and selling some pieces in our silent auction." She seemed animated now—almost excited.

"Dana Coons and Nicole Hemingway will be there. Dana does those lovely paintings of children." Mrs. Ames waved a hand toward the large portrait of two small children playing in the sand. "I commissioned her to do that one from an old photograph of Jessica and Micky."

"It's beautiful." Gram studied the painting, then glanced over at Mrs. Ames, who'd moved over to an ornate teapot in blacks, browns, and an iridescent copper and green. "And this is one of Nicole's raku works." Without waiting for a response, she went to the sea-green sculpture of a mermaid swimming in a spiral—her hair flowing behind. Mrs. Ames slid her hand down the mermaid's smooth back and tail.

"Eric Meyers," Gram said. "I'd love to have one of his pieces. As for coming to the benefit, I'll have to check with J.B."

"Your new husband. I'd love to meet him."

"If we don't come Wednesday night, I'll be sure to bring him over sometime soon."

Jennie entered the room, and for a moment neither woman spoke.

"There you are, darling," Gram said. "Are you ready to go?"

Mrs. Ames looked Jennie's way. "Of course you must bring Jennie as well."

*More than ready.* Jennie tossed the silent message to Gram, then asked, "Bring me to what?"

"The benefit," Mrs. Ames responded. "Each year we feature a different artist's work at an auction to raise money for the Coastal Arts Association. Actually, this year we're turning it into a fund-raiser to earn money to keep gambling out of Bay Village. You really should come. All three artists said they were doing something special to honor Jessica."

"Jessica knew them?" Jennie asked.

"Oh yes. She studied art this summer and spent a couple weeks working under each of them."

Jennie made up her mind to go but didn't say so. She'd have to clear it with Gram. They thanked Mrs. Ames and within a few minutes were on their way.

"She seems nice," Jennie said. "But strange."

"In what way?" Gram snapped her seat belt in place and started the car.

Jennie shrugged. "Earlier when we were talking about Jessica, she looked ready to cry—and just now, it was like nothing happened. How could she switch like that?"

"Oh, I have a feeling all of this art business is her way of coping. She's doing what a lot of people do after they lose a loved one—trying to stay busy and concentrate on other things."

"Hmm." Jennie paused to wave at Micky and Don as they arranged a ramp in the driveway to practice jumps with their skateboards. Glancing back at Gram she asked, "Did you do that when Grandpa Ian died?" Gram's first husband had been a government agent assigned to a special task force in the Middle East when the building he'd been working in was bombed.

"I sure did—for a while. I worked a little too hard. Then I sort of checked out for a while."

"I don't remember that."

Gram smiled. "No one knew. Except maybe Kate and your father. I went on a cruise and started writing. It took a long time to get to where I could function normally again."

"So you think Mrs. Ames is acting normal?"

"For someone who's lost a child there is no normal."

"What was she like before?"

"I don't know her that well." Gram turned left onto the main highway. "She entertains quite a bit—seems I'm always getting invitations to social functions. Most of them are political. The mayor likes to entertain too."

"You sound like you don't especially like him."

"He's nice enough. I just don't happen to agree with him on certain political issues."

"Like?"

"Abortion for one. I'm an advocate for children—even those who haven't been born. He's pro-choice. He's also a member of the National Rifle Association, and while he's willing to look at some reforms regarding gun control, he doesn't go far enough in my opinion. We do agree on some things—like environmental issues and gambling. He's against the initiative to bring a Vegas-style casino to Bay Village."

Jennie told her about the book she'd found in Jessica's room and Mrs. Ames' response to it. "About the only people Mrs. Ames could think of that Jessica might be helping were Todd or his brother."

"Interesting. Of course Todd is underage, but looks old-enough—it's possible. More likely, though, it would be Greg. I didn't realize he had a problem in that area, but then I don't know the family all that well. Annie Costello is a cousin, so all I know about the boys is what she tells me from time to time."

Jennie turned in her seat and rested the back of her head against the window. "What did she tell you?"

"The boys lost their father about ten years ago. Tragic accident in the woods. Mr. Kopelund was a logger. His brother—Annie's father—worked with him and lost the use of both legs. Annie, bless her heart, not only had to care for her invalid father but took the boys in as well. Greg was only fifteen at the time, and though they received a small pension, it wasn't enough for them to live on. He quit school and went to work on a fishing boat."

"Oh, Gram, that's so sad. Do you think losing his dad messed him up?"

"Hmm. I do get the feeling Greg resents his lot in life—which is a tragedy in itself. Eventually, Annie was able to leave her father with a caregiver part time and develop her catering business. And Greg worked very hard to build his business. He and Todd moved into a place of their own three or four years ago. He does quite well for himself."

"What does he do?"

"Takes tourists out on fishing and whale-watching excursions. He has three boats now, and Todd works with him. That's about all I can tell you. Maybe Ryan can give you more information."

Jennie groaned. "Ryan . . . he's probably furious with me by now."

"Relax, darling. I told him what happened before I came to pick you up. He wants you to call him when you get in."

Gram pulled into Orcas Lane. Bernie bounded out to meet them, followed by Nick and Ryan.

"Hey, guys, did you miss me?" Jennie asked.

"Yay! Jennie's here." Nick leapt into Jennie's arms, and Bernie nearly knocked her down. Ryan stood back a few feet, his jaw set, his arms crossed.

When Nick and Bernie turned their attention to Gram, Jennie walked over to him. "Sorry I'm late."

"I thought we were going over to the Ameses' together."

"I . . . um . . . I didn't mean to go there." She sighed. "I'll explain later. Did you still want to go?"

"No. Let's go see Todd."

"Sure. Hang on while I get my keys."

After telling Gram where she was going and making sure it was okay to leave Nick, they set off in Jennie's Mustang. When they reached the main road, Ryan asked, "Did you find anything?"

Jennie quickly filled him in on her adventure—finding the ring, the book, and her conversation with Jessica's mom.

"So Mrs. Ames thinks Todd is into gambling. I can't believe she'd tell you that. It's not true."

"What about Greg?"

Ryan hesitated a moment too long. "He goes to the casino once in a while. But Todd's never said anything about it being a problem or anything."

"Could Jessica have been trying to talk to Todd about his

brother's problem?" Jennie's gaze drifted to Ryan, then back to the road.

"Maybe, but what would that have to do with Jessica's murder?"

"I'm not sure it does. Jessica and Todd could have gotten into an argument over it and—"

Ryan's angry gaze collided with hers. "You think Todd killed Jessica because Greg gambles a little?"

"I didn't say that." Jennie turned into the parking lot of the municipal building.

"No, but you were thinking it."

"How do you know what I'm thinking?"

"I can see it in your eyes and the expression you get when we talk about it. You think Todd killed her."

"Ryan . . ." Jennie brought her volume down a few notches.

Ryan didn't. "Save the explanations. I thought I could count on you to help me clear Todd, but I was wrong."

Jennie pulled into a parking space and braked a little harder than necessary. "That's not fair. I'm just trying to be objective. I don't know if Todd killed her or not."

"He didn't!" Ryan released his seat belt and climbed out of the car. Slamming the door shut, he leaned through the open window. "Maybe it would be better if you didn't come in with me to see Todd right now. Thanks for the ride. I'll find my own way home."

Stunned, Jennie stared at Ryan's back as he walked away. Part of her felt like running after him and trying to explain. Another part wanted to punch him. *There's no point going after him*, she told herself. Ryan seemed totally convinced of Todd's innocence. While Jennie wished she could side with him, she couldn't—not yet. Maybe not ever.

# 7

"Back so soon?" Gram looked up, then turned her attention back to the baking dish and the big salmon filet inside it.

"Ryan hates me." Jennie slumped into one of the kitchen chairs and watched Gram peel a clove of garlic. "I didn't say a thing, and he's convinced I think Todd is guilty. He won't listen to me."

"Hmm, a rather strong reaction coming from Ryan. I wonder if maybe he's having some doubts about his friend."

"Are you kidding? He's absolutely, positively, one-hundred-percent certain that Todd is innocent."

"So he says. My hunch is that he may not be so sure, and his uncertainty is making him angry with himself."

"Then why is he mad at me?"

Gram squeezed fresh lemon over the fish, then sprinkled on a bunch of diced garlic. "Human behavior can be rather complicated where emotions are concerned. And of course I can't say for certain, but Ryan may be aiming his anger at you because you're willing to accept something he can't."

"That makes no sense to me. All I know is he's being a jerk." Jennie unfolded herself from the chair. "Do you want me to help with dinner?"

Gram handed her an onion. "You could slice this for me. We'll put about half of it on the fish."

The tears came as Jennie sliced. Onions always made her cry, but she was glad for the cover. Her anger with Ryan was turning into a huge weight in her chest.

"Oh, Gram," Jennie sobbed. "What am I gonna do? I can't tell Ryan I agree with him about Todd. I'd be lying. There's a lot of evidence against him. And I may have found more." Jennie paused to mop up her tears, then blubbered on about the ring and her suspicion that Jessica may have been trying to break up with him. "Maybe she was handing the ring back, and they argued . . . then he pushed her."

"Or she could have lost the ring days before she died. Did Mrs. Ames say how Jessica felt about Todd?"

"Only that Jessica never took her ring off—which reminds me, I forgot to give it back to Mrs. Ames. Oh well, I should turn it over to the authorities anyway." Jennie grabbed a couple tissues to deal with the rest of her tears, then went to the sink to wash her hands. "I'm going to talk to some other people Jessica knew." Remembering the picture on Jessica's dresser, Jennie asked, "Do you know a girl named Camilla? I think she might be a friend of Jessica's."

"Camilla." Gram stared at the ceiling as if she might find the answer there, then shifted her gaze back to Jennie. "Matt and Nancy Daniels have a daughter named Camilla—yes, she's probably about the right age."

"Where do they live?"

"I'm not sure—in Lincoln City, I think. They run the Whale and Dolphin Gift Shop & Bakery in downtown Bay Village. In fact, Camilla may work for them."

"She does." Jennie's memory of where she'd seen the girl in the picture snapped into place. "Thanks, Gram. I knew I'd seen her somewhere." Jennie dried her hands and glanced at her watch. She couldn't catch Camilla today. The stores in Bay Village closed at five, and it was now ten after. She considered calling first but decided a drop-in visit might be better.

Jennie's tears had dried up from the onions and from her disappointment with Ryan. While the salmon baked, Jennie made the salad and set the table.

The baked salmon—one of Jennie's favorites—turned out perfect, but then it always did when Gram made it. J.B. and Nick arrived in time for dinner. The good food and companionable conversation with Gram, her new grandfather, and Nick made Jennie almost forget about her argument with Ryan. In fact, she might have done just fine if Ryan hadn't come over at seven-thirty to see her.

Feelings of frustration and anger mingled with excitement bubbled up all over again when he rang the doorbell. She thought seriously of having Gram tell him she didn't want to talk to him, but she didn't. Truth was, she did want to see him—very much. Jennie swallowed back her injured pride and met him at the door.

"Hi." Ryan's blue eyes met hers. He leaned against the door jamb, acting like nothing had happened. "Um . . . I wondered if you wanted to go down on the rocks and watch the sunset."

Jennie couldn't quite bring herself to say no, but she didn't want to seem too eager either. "I guess." She slipped back inside to get her jacket, then, stuffing her hands in her pockets, joined him on the porch. They walked most of the way to the rocks without speaking.

"Supposed to be warm tomorrow," Ryan said.

Jennie didn't answer.

"Would you like to go to Newport with me? We could go to the aquarium and maybe walk on the beach."

Normally Jennie would have been thrilled with the invitation, but their relationship had slipped too far, and Jennie wasn't sure she wanted to spend the day with him—at least not unless he was willing to apologize. "I thought you were mad at me."

"I am—about Todd. But we shouldn't let a difference of

opinion keep us from being friends."

Jennie stopped. Ryan took four steps before he realized she wasn't beside him, then turned around and came back. "What's wrong?"

"I'm not sure what you're trying to say, Ryan. A friend doesn't act like you did today. You wouldn't even listen to me."

Ryan tipped back on his heels and sighed. "I . . . I know. And I'm sorry about that. It's making me crazy. I wish there were something I could do. If we could find one shred of evidence that would clear him. I was hoping you could help, but . . . so far all you've done is make things look worse for him."

"Not on purpose. I'm not going out to deliberately prove Todd killed Jessica. I just want to know the truth. Don't you?"

Jennie started walking again, and Ryan fell into step beside her. "I guess, but what if all the evidence points to Todd? I know he didn't do it."

"See, that's the problem. What if he's lying to you?"

"I don't think he is."

Jennie shrugged. "Okay, say he's telling the truth. Then the real killer must be planting evidence to pin the crime on Todd. What we need to find out is who. Who would want Jessica dead? And why?"

"I can't think of anyone. I guess that's what's so frustrating to me. I keep looking for a reason. Everyone liked Jessica. Well, maybe not everyone. Todd sometimes thought she should mind her own business—she was kind of an activist. Got involved in political issues."

"Like?"

"Environmental stuff. She and her mom put on a couple of big benefits to bring Keiko up to Oregon. And she tied herself to a tree once. But I can't think of anyone who'd be upset with her for that."

"What about this gambling thing? If she's against it—"

"I doubt Jessica's influence is broad enough to make a difference." Ryan took her hand to help her over a wide crack in the rocks. "I'm against the gambling, too, my entire family is—in fact, most of the people in my church are. The only really influential people opposed to the gambling are Mayor Ames, Senator Baker, and Judge Crookston, but you don't see anyone going after them."

"Unless—" Jennie stopped herself. The idea was too far-fetched. Bay Village was much too small. Still, it was something to consider. What if someone wanted gambling in Bay Village badly enough to kill? What if Jessica was murdered because she was the mayor's daughter?

"What were you going to say?" Ryan slipped an arm around her shoulders.

"Never mind." Jennie set the bizarre thought aside and changed the subject. "Gram says maybe you got mad at me because you're having doubts about Todd."

His eyebrows almost met when he frowned. "She might be right. I want to believe Todd, and I do, but . . . I don't know. You really threw me with that business about the ring and the gambling. I asked Todd about it. He said he doesn't gamble and swears he never talked to Jessica about Greg. He also told me Jessica was wearing the ring the last time he saw her."

"How can you be sure he's telling the truth?"

"I trust him, Jen—he's my friend. Anyway, let's not talk about Jessica or Todd right now." Ryan turned to face her and pulled her close.

"What do you want to talk about?" Her voice sounded strange and breathless.

"At the moment, nothing."

One light kiss on the lips and she almost managed to put the case out of her mind. Another and it faded to a distant memory.

The next morning, Jennie woke up daydreaming abut Ryan. They'd watched the sunset together and talked about the future—school, mostly, and what they hoped to do after graduation and college. True to his word, Ryan hadn't mentioned Jessica or Todd. Jennie had enjoyed their time together, but something had changed. As much as she wanted to deny it, she could still feel the tension between them. Ryan seemed farther away than ever.

The door creaked open. Jennie flopped onto her stomach and pulled the covers over her head.

"C'mon, Jennie." Nick ran in and climbed up on the bed and onto her back.

"Ouch, Nick," Jennie groaned. "I don't feel like playing horsey this morning. Go away."

"Gram said I'm s'posed to wake you up for breakfast." He kept bouncing.

How anyone could have that much energy at seven in the morning was completely beyond Jennie's comprehension. She managed to turn onto her back between bounces and reel him in. "Hold still for a minute. I want to ask you something."

"What?" Nick snuggled up against her and looked at her nose-to-nose, his big navy blue eyes only inches away.

Jennie chuckled as they rubbed noses. "How come you're so rambunctious this morning?"

"I'm not ra-bun-chus, I'm adorable—Gram said so." He climbed off the bed. "Gram said I should tell you she made blueberry pancakes. I gotta go get some."

"I'll be down in a minute. Don't forget to feed Bernie."

"Papa and me already did."

After taking a quick shower, Jennie pulled on jeans and a navy sweat shirt sporting a picture of whales and the words *Oregon Coast*.

She and Ryan would be heading to Newport at nine-thirty. That gave her exactly two hours to eat and go into town to talk to Camilla.

———

At eight, Jennie pulled up in front of the Whale and Dolphin Gift Shop & Bakery. The wind blew a cold rain against her windshield. Jennie took a deep breath and raced for the covered wooden porch of the old Victorian house turned gift shop. Mrs. Daniels opened the door with a cheery good-morning.

Jennie introduced herself. "Is Camilla here?"

"Not yet." Mrs. Daniels turned her closed sign around to read open. "She'll be here in about fifteen minutes. You're welcome to wait."

Jennie glanced around trying to decide whether to hang around or come back. She decided to stay. She'd already eaten breakfast but ordered a cranberry scone and a cup of herbal tea anyway, then settled into a chair near the window.

At eight-fifteen, Jennie watched Camilla pull up in a white Toyota. The wind whipped through her short, curly blond hair as she climbed out of the car.

The door to the shop flew open when she grasped the handle, and Camilla released a bird-like squeal, then pushed the door against the wind.

"Looks like it's getting nasty out there." Mrs. Daniels looked over the counter.

"Typical." Camilla pulled off her Windbreaker and headed for a room behind the counter. She emerged seconds later wearing a white apron over her pale yellow shirt and faded blue jeans.

"Mom, would you mind if I leave early today? I'm going out with this really great guy tonight."

"Really? You sound excited."

"I am. I've been waiting two years for him to notice me."

"Do I know him?"

"I think so." Camilla hugged herself and twirled around. "It's Ryan Johnson."

# 8

Jennie gasped, sucked a piece of scone down her windpipe, and went into a coughing fit. When she could finally talk, Camilla and Mrs. Daniels were hovering over her. Not that she cared. At the moment she wished they'd go away and let her suffer in peace. Ryan and Camilla—if she weren't so frantically trying to clear her trachea, she'd be racing to her car. And the tears in her eyes would be for Ryan instead of a result of the choking.

"Are you all right?" Mrs. Daniels patted her on the back. "Camilla, get her some water."

Camilla hurried off and came back a few moments later. Jennie drank several swallows and tried to clear her throat for the umpteenth time.

"What happened?" Camilla asked.

Jennie shook her head. "Swallowed wrong. I'm okay." She wasn't, of course. Camilla's announcement about her date with Ryan hurt far more than the crumbs in her throat. She couldn't decide whether to cry or throw a fit. Jennie did neither. She had to concentrate on why she'd come.

"You're sure you're okay?" Mrs. Daniels hunkered down in front of her. "Maybe some more hot tea will help. Can I get you a refill?"

"Yes, please." Jennie wanted nothing more than to escape, but she'd come to talk to Camilla and wasn't about to

58

leave without some answers. The tea would help soothe her throat and hopefully settle the chaos churning inside.

"I'll get it." Camilla started to get up, but Mrs. Daniels stopped her. "Stay. Jennie's been waiting to talk with you."

Camilla's questioning blue-green gaze drifted to Jennie. "You have?"

Jennie nodded, then cleared her throat. After introducing herself, she added, "I wanted to ask you some questions about Jessica."

Camilla slid into the chair across from Jennie, her features shifting from concern to sadness. "Why?"

Jennie could hardly mention that Ryan had asked her to investigate Jessica's murder. "It's hard to explain. I saw your picture in Jessica's room, and I knew you worked here." She paused when the bell tinkled and a couple walked in. They wandered over to the pastry window and drooled over the selections.

Mrs. Daniels brought a fresh pot of water and a tea bag and set it down in front of Jennie, then went to wait on her customers.

"Why do you want to know?" Camilla folded her arms and leaned over the table.

"A friend of mine thinks the police have the wrong person in jail and . . ."

"Oh, I do too. Poor Todd. It's all so terrible and unnecessary. I don't believe Todd killed Jessica—I don't think anyone did."

"Then what. . . ?"

Camilla leaned closer. "I think she killed herself."

"Suicide?" Jennie had wondered about that possibility herself. "What do the police say?"

Camilla looked at a car pulling into the parking lot and sighed. "They thought so at first, but the coroner ruled out suicide because of the position of the body, some scratches, and because she was holding a shirt in her hand."

"Todd's shirt?"

"Yes." Her gaze shifted back to Jennie. "But that doesn't mean anything. He could have loaned it to her. She liked wearing guy's shirts over her tank tops. Anyway, Jessica was really depressed the day she died, and it wasn't about Todd."

"You saw her that day?" Jennie swirled her peppermint tea bag in the water and lifted it, watching the green-tinged liquid drip back into the cup. Normally she would have made eye contact. Unfortunately, whenever she looked into Camilla's eyes she thought of Ryan looking into them. He had a lot of explaining to do.

"A couple of times. She came into the shop in the morning to get some bakery stuff for her mom and some artist friends they were having over for coffee. I stopped by after work for a few minutes. She was upset about something but wouldn't tell me. It couldn't have been about Todd because she'd have talked to me about that—I mean, like if she were breaking up with him. She always told me about Todd."

Jennie pulled the ring off her finger and held it out to Camilla. "Have you ever seen this before?"

"Where did you get that?"

"On the rocks by where Jessica's body was found. It had lodged in a crack. Mrs. Ames says Todd gave it to Jessica."

"He did. It's a promise ring. They loved each other and wanted to get married someday, and the ring was a promise to each other that they'd stay pure—you know—abstain from sex."

"Was she wearing it the last time you saw her alive?"

"Yes." Camilla frowned. "I'm sure she was. She had this little habit of twisting it around on her finger. That's how I knew she was really nervous. She kept turning it and pulling it on and off."

"But she didn't say anything about giving it back to Todd?"

"No." Camilla pinched her lips together. Tears gathered

in her eyes. She grabbed a napkin and dabbed at them.

The bell above the door jingled. Two women came in and headed for the counter. Camilla excused herself to go wait on them.

Jennie thought about staying and asking her about Ryan. *What good would that do?* she asked herself. *The one you need to talk to is Ryan.*

She tucked Jessica's ring in her pocket, mumbled a hasty thank-you and good-bye, then left.

————

Jennie pulled into Gram's driveway at nine-forty-five—half an hour later than when she'd planned to be back. The trip from town to Gram's normally took five minutes. Jennie had spent the other twenty-five sitting in her car overlooking the ocean. She'd watched the rain slam against her windshield, blurring her view. She'd practiced over and over what to say to Ryan. Without crying.

Ryan jogged across the yard toward her, pulled open the passenger side door, then folded himself into the seat. "I was getting worried about you. I thought we were leaving at nine-thirty."

Jennie glanced at him, then back at the sky. She focused on the small swatch of blue between the clouds, but it was far too close to the color of Ryan's eyes. "I'm not going."

"Why? What's the matter? Are you sick or something?"

"I guess you could say that."

"What's wrong?"

Jennie took a deep breath and steeled herself to meet his gaze. "I went to see Camilla Daniels this morning."

"Why didn't you tell me? I'd have gone with you." His blue eyes showed no sign of guilt. "What did she say?"

Jennie gripped the steering wheel. "About you or Todd?"

"Todd, of course. Why would she say anything about me?" As if remembering something important Ryan closed his eyes and tipped his head back against the seat. "Oh man." He drew both hands down his face. "She told you we were having dinner?"

"Not exactly." Jennie glanced at Ryan, taking small comfort in his embarrassment. "She didn't say where you were going or what you were doing. Only that she'd been waiting for two years for you to notice her."

"Jennie, Camilla is a friend. The only reason I'm seeing her is to ask her about Jessica. I was going to ask you to come along."

Remembering the excitement in Camilla's voice, Jennie doubted it. "Yeah, right. You need me to drive."

"I swear, Jennie—"

"Save it. I saw the look in her eyes when she came into the store this morning. You might think of her as a friend, but she doesn't think of you that way." Jennie looked away from him again, remembering back to her own friendship with Ryan. Maybe that's all she was to him too. He'd said he loved her once, but that had been months ago. He'd kissed her the night before—twice, but he'd said nothing about love.

Ryan reached for the door handle. "What do you want me to do, cancel? I'll do that if it will make you happy."

Jennie cringed at the hard edge in his voice. *Yes, call her, tell her you changed your mind. Tell her you're going out with me instead.* She wanted to say the words but couldn't. "The only thing that will make me happy right now is for you to get out of my car and leave me alone."

"Fine." He jerked open the door and climbed out. "I'm not going to argue with you. I'm sorry you won't believe me."

"I believe what I see."

He leaned over and caught her faltering gaze. Rain pelted his face and dripped from his eyelashes onto his cheeks. "If you want to come with me to talk to Camilla, be at my house by six-thirty. Otherwise I'm going without you." He slammed the door and stalked down the driveway to his house.

Jennie placed her arms across the steering wheel and rested her head against her forearms. The fact that Ryan still planned to see Camilla was proof enough that he was interested in her. And who wouldn't be? Camilla was cute, and she believed in Todd's innocence. They had at least that in common. Ryan didn't have to take Camilla to dinner to get information. He could have just gone to see her, like Jennie had. Or he could have asked Jennie what she'd found out.

*You're better off without him,* she told herself. *Anyway, it isn't like you're engaged. You never agreed not to go out with other people.* Ryan's words from the day before marched through her brain like tiny soldiers standing at attention. *"I don't want this thing with Todd to ruin our friendship."* Friendship. Not relationship. He'd been clear enough about that. Yet he'd kissed her like he cared. *Just forget it.* Jennie jerked open the car door and stormed into the house. She stomped on the rug, as much to deal with her anger as to shake off the rain.

The house was empty. A note on the kitchen table told Jennie that Gram and J.B. had taken Nick to Lincoln City for the day. They'd be staying in town for dinner. Jennie went to the refrigerator and stared unseeing at its contents. She retrieved a can of Diet Coke and a handful of peeled baby carrots. Popping the top of the can, she went into the living room and flopped onto the couch.

Great. Just what she needed—an entire day to herself. Jennie vacillated between feeling sorry for herself and being grateful for the time alone. Once she'd drained her drink and crunched the carrots, she had a better perspective on things. She tucked her argument with Ryan aside. Time would tell if he was telling the truth. Maybe he did think of Camilla as just a friend. Maybe not. Jennie thought about taking Ryan up on his offer to go along with him when he met Camilla. She wouldn't, she decided. It would be too uncomfortable for all of them—especially for Camilla.

In the meantime, she'd use her unexpected gift of time to

concentrate on Jessica Ames' death. There were a lot of other people to talk to and no time like now to make plans. On a fresh sheet of paper, Jennie began listing the names. Mayor Ames, Annie, Greg, the three artists, and Jessica's brother, Micky. And of course, Todd. She looked the list over again, then folded it and tucked it into the back pocket of her jeans. Too many people—so little time.

Jennie took her can to the kitchen and dumped it in the recycling bin, then grabbed the phone book. She ran her finger down the Lincoln County listings and picked up the phone.

"Municipal building," the crisp male voice answered.

"Hi." Jennie swallowed back the anxiety rising like a flock of frightened swallows from the pit of her stomach. "Could you tell me when visiting hours are? I'd like to come to the jail to see Todd Kopelund."

# 9

Todd was wearing the same scared look he'd had in the courtroom. Jennie sat at a table opposite him. He rested his handcuffed wrists on the scarred wooden table and leaned toward her. "I sure didn't expect to see you," he said, his deep brown eyes assessing her.

"Why?" Jennie lifted a pad of paper out of her backpack.

"I don't know—just didn't. Why are you here?"

"I'm curious. Ryan thinks I should hear your side of the story."

"Funny—he didn't think you were interested. What if I don't feel like telling you?"

"Then don't." She pushed her chair back.

"Wait." His broad shoulders sagged as his gaze dropped to his hands. "I'm sorry. It's just that things are looking pretty hopeless. The evidence is stacked against me, but I didn't do it. I loved Jessica. I wouldn't do anything to hurt her. I wish people could believe that."

"Was she breaking up with you?"

"No." He glanced up at Jennie, then looked away.

Watching his expression, Jennie pulled the ring out of her pocket and explained where she'd found it. "Any idea how it got down on the rocks?"

"No."

Jennie didn't believe him. She had a hard time seeing him

as a killer, but she didn't trust him either.

"Why was she holding your shirt?"

"I have no idea—look, she said she was cold, okay? I loaned it to her and said she could give it back later."

"Lying isn't going to help your case, Todd. Maybe if you'd tell the truth—"

"Truth?" His nostrils flared. "These people don't care about the truth. Jessica's father is out for blood—mine. He's the one who's lying."

Jennie arched an eyebrow in disbelief. "Why would Mayor Ames lie?"

Todd leaned closer, glanced at the guard by the door, then whispered, "Maybe he's been paid to protect the real killer. Or maybe someone is threatening to kill him or another member of the family. I wouldn't be surprised is he isn't paying off the sheriff and the D.A. to make sure I take the blame. He's made some powerful enemies coming out against the gambling bill."

Chewing on the inside of her cheek, Jennie held back her skeptical response. Not that she intended to write off his comments—she didn't. In fact, the idea intrigued her, and she'd make it a point to find out as much about the mayor as possible. Todd's accusations were in line with what she had been thinking earlier—that maybe someone had gotten to the mayor through his daughter.

"You really believe Jessica's death has something to do with the gambling issue?" Jennie asked.

"I told you I did."

"Mrs. Ames said you might have talked to Jessica about Greg's gambling problem. Is it possible she might have confronted him and—"

"What are you saying? You think my brother killed her?" Todd's handcuffs clunked against the table when he stood. The guard moved closer, resting his hand on his weapon.

Todd's hot gaze shifted back and forth between the guard and Jennie.

Todd retreated back to his chair, his anger dissipating like fire in water. The guard moved a discreet distance away.

Jennie rose from the table and hooked her backpack over her shoulder. Maybe coming to see Todd hadn't been a such a wise decision. "I'd better go."

"My brother didn't do anything wrong." Todd heaved a deep sigh. "He gambles sometimes, but not that much. Anyway, even if Jessica did talk to him, he'd have no reason to kill her."

"How does he feel about bringing gambling into Bay Village?"

"He's for the initiative, but—" Todd frowned. "Look, Jennie, Greg doesn't care if Bay Village gets a casino. He can always drive up to the Soaring Eagle or into Lincoln City. If you really want to find out who killed Jessica, talk to the people who stand to lose the most if the bill is defeated."

"Any idea who that might be?" Jennie pushed the chair in and remained standing.

"The guys who want to build it. The developers. Whoever put up the money for the campaign."

"Can you give me any names?"

"No. But Greg might be able to."

Jennie adjusted the strap on her bag. "Thanks. I'll talk to him. Do you know where I might find him?"

"He's probably out fishing right now. He'll be down on the docks later—around four. Look for the *Linda Sue*. He'll either be there or on one of the two boats in the slips beside her."

Jennie nodded. "Todd . . ."

"What?"

Jennie waited until his gaze met hers before speaking. "About the ring."

Todd closed his eyes. "I took Jessica home around ten

that night. She was wearing the ring then."

"The paper said Mayor Ames saw you pull out of the driveway around midnight."

"I don't know who he saw, but it wasn't me."

On her way out, Jennie stopped by the office to ask where she might find the sheriff. The deputy grinned up at her. "You're in luck, young lady. Sheriff Adams just walked in."

"Adams? As in Joe?" Jennie turned toward the door and the sound of footsteps in the marble entry.

"Jennie!" Joe Adams flashed her a wide grin. "It's great to see you." He turned to the man at the desk and made the introductions. "Jennie is Helen Bradley's granddaughter."

"That so?" The clerk nodded in approval, then turned back to answer the ringing phone.

"Did you want to see me about something?" Joe asked, motioning toward one of two offices to their right.

"Yeah." Jennie went in ahead of him and sat down. Something about Joe always flustered her. Maybe it was his movie-star face—or the way his dark eyes captured hers as if he were trying to read something written on her soul.

She waited until he was seated, then asked, "So how's the arm?" The last time she'd seen Joe he'd been shot. Jennie had been credited with saving his life.

"Great. I'm still doing therapy, but I was able to come back to work the first of the month."

"That's good."

"You didn't come in just to ask about my health."

"Um . . . no." She fished the ring out of her pocket and handed it to him. "This was Jessica's—I found it on the rocks by where she fell."

He scrutinized the ring, then set it on the desk blotter in front of him. "How do you know it's Jessica's?"

"Her mom and best friend *and* Todd identified it."

"Hmm. I appreciate your bringing it in, but in the future you might want to turn over evidence right away and let us do the investigating. Is there anything else I should know?"

"Maybe." Joe's steady gaze kept Jennie talking until she'd told him everything she'd said and done in the last few days, including her argument with Ryan.

When she finished, Joe leaned back in his chair and clasped his hands behind his neck.

Jennie cleared her throat, feeling pinned like a specimen under a microscope. She looked away, then back again. "Why don't you say something?"

He straightened and tapped his fingers on the desk. "Any idea how the ring ended up on the rocks?"

"The only thing I can think of is that Jessica broke up with him—maybe they argued and she threw the ring away."

"Do you think Todd is guilty?"

"Huh?"

"You heard me."

"Yeah . . . I just didn't expect—" Jennie sighed. "I don't know. Ryan doesn't think so. I'm not so sure."

"I'm not either. We've got the evidence and a couple of eyewitnesses that put him at the scene at the appropriate time, but something about this isn't ringing true."

Jennie didn't know how to respond. She'd expected to be yelled at and warned away, but she certainly hadn't expected Joe to take her into his confidence. "What's that?"

"Motive. As it stands now, we really don't have one—unless Jessica did break up with him. You're not the only one with that theory, by the way. The mayor suspects that as well. If your suspicions are true, that still leaves us with a big question—did he kill her?"

"They could have fought, and he could have pushed her," Jennie surmised.

"It's possible. He's got a history of getting hot-headed, but according to Annie and Greg and some of his friends, he's never come to blows with anyone." He shook his head. "It's a real puzzle."

"It could have been an accident." Jennie recounted her near disaster with Ryan on the rocks.

"Could be, but why would Todd lie about it? What would you have done if Ryan had fallen?"

"I'd have tried to save him."

"Exactly. I think if Todd had been there he'd have called for help and gone down to try to save her. I can't see him leaving her like that."

"What about the possibility of suicide?"

"We've pretty much ruled that out. She'd definitely struggled with someone before she fell." He picked up the ring and studied it again, then set it down.

His dark brows drew together. "Jessica may have been killed by someone wanting to silence her—or her father. If my hunch is right, and someone other than Todd killed Jessica, I'd just as soon not have you or Ryan snooping around."

Without waiting for a response, Joe rose and came around to the front of his desk and leaned against it. "I could get hard-nosed at this point and order you to stay out of the investigation. I'm not going to do that, but I am going to ask for your cooperation."

If his plan had been to intimidate her, it was working. "Sure. How can I help?"

"As far as the press and anyone else is concerned, we've got our killer. No one, outside of yourself and a few law enforcement people I'm working with, knows I'm not convinced of Todd's guilt. I'd just as soon keep it that way for a while."

"So the real killer won't feel threatened?"

"Among other things. I don't want you kids out there asking questions and stirring things up. The last thing I need is another murder."

Jennie swallowed back the rising concern that she or Ryan had already asked too many questions. "That's okay with me.

I think you'd better have a talk with Ryan, though. He's determined to prove Todd didn't do it."

Joe sighed and glanced heavenward. "I used to think amateur detectives only made life miserable for cops in books and on television."

Jennie's lips shifted to form a smile. "At least you don't have to worry about Gram. She's too busy writing to get involved in this one."

"Actually, I think of your grandmother as one of us. She's helped the department solve a number of cases. The thing is, Jennie—and I can't stress this enough—we're not playing games here. You can rest assured the investigation is in good hands. Besides the local authorities, we've got the FBI involved. I'll talk to Ryan, but in the meantime I need your promise that you'll leave Jessica's murder investigation to me."

"The FBI? Why would they be involved?"

Joe folded his arms across his chest. "There's a possibility we're dealing with organized crime. They're looking into Vegas connections. Like I said, Jennie, it's best if you stay out of it."

Jennie agreed and felt a rush of relief at the thought of not being involved anymore. Now maybe she could relax and enjoy the rest of her vacation—even if she did have to spend it without Ryan. She loved being with her family, and she should be spending more time with Nick anyway.

Jennie wished Joe luck and left the office, then maneuvered her Mustang out of the gravel parking lot onto the highway.

Back at Gram's, Jennie started a fire in the fireplace and was just settling down on the couch to read when the doorbell rang. Grumbling, she hurried to answer it. No one was there. Only her Mustang sat in the driveway. Whoever had been there must have been on foot. Ryan?

She leaned out and looked toward his house. Rustling

leaves and a movement of bushes to the right brought hairs on Jennie's neck to attention. She slammed the door shut and slid the deadbolt lock into place.

Jennie had one terrifying thought. The sheriff's warning to mind her own business may have come too late. What if some hit man had been sent to kill her? Her heart thundering, Jennie ran to the other entry to make certain that door was locked as well. Not that locking it would help. If someone wanted to get in, all they had to do was break the glass.

Jennie methodically checked the windows, closed the blinds, and retreated to the couch. After a few minutes, she began to feel foolish. The noise may have been an animal or a bird. Determined not to be scared out of her wits, Jennie took a deep breath and ventured outside.

# 10

"All right, guys." Jennie scooped up a skateboard and parted the wet bushes. "Come on out." It hadn't taken long to figure out the source of the noise.

"I told ya we shouldn't have hid." Micky Ames crept out on all fours, followed by his friend Don. "It was his fault. He wanted to talk to you and then chickened out."

"I did not—I mean, he's the one that chickened out." Don's cheeks had turned a vibrant rose, and it wasn't entirely from the cold.

Jennie handed Don his skateboard. "Do you two want to come inside?"

They hesitated until Jennie offered hot chocolate. She hung their dripping jackets in the entry, then led the way to the kitchen. Once they were seated around the table, steaming cups in hand, Jennie asked the obvious question. "What did you want to talk to me about?"

Micky licked the chocolate mustache from his upper lip and glanced at his friend. "Don likes you. He wanted to see if you'd come to the party with him."

Don rolled his eyes. "Don't listen to him, Jennie. He's being a dork. He's the one that wanted you to come to the party. We just thought we could get you in easier if I brought you."

"What party?"

"The benefit my mom and dad are having," Micky replied.

"Um—guys, I'm flattered, really, but I think I'm a little too old—"

"It's not like a date," Micky said. "We just want you to come 'cause maybe you can help us find out who killed Jessica."

Jennie wagged her head back and forth. "Whoa. You've got the wrong girl. I'm not—"

"But you have to." Micky set his cup down as if to emphasize his point. "See, we know Todd didn't hurt Jessica, and we don't think it's fair that he's in jail."

"Do you have proof?"

"No, but you could help us find it."

This was getting downright weird. Why did everyone think she could prove anything? "I don't think so. The person you really need to be talking to is the sheriff."

"Give her the book," Don said.

Jennie looked from one to the other.

Micky got up and withdrew a small, cloth-covered book from the pocket of his baggy pants. He set it on the table and slid it toward Jennie.

"What's this?"

"Jessica's diary. There are pages missing, but Don and me figured out some of it."

Jennie stared at the book. "You should take it to Sheriff Adams."

The floral design seemed to draw her hand forward. She didn't mean to open it, but she couldn't stop herself. The entries started at the beginning of summer. She noted Todd's name often and Camilla's. Nothing out of the ordinary until she came to where the writing stopped. Her last entry ended with *Todd and I went out again tonight and*

The next two pages had been ripped out.

Micky came around behind her and pointed to the rough edges in the book's crease. "We could see that something had been written there so we used a pencil and scribbled over it.

You can see part of what she wrote."

The pencil shading had revealed what may have been Jessica's final message to the world.

*I can't believe he'd do something like this. I'm going to talk to him tonight. It's late—almost midnight, but I need to know the truth. . . . I hear a car . . . he's back.*

Micky went back to his chair. "We know she wasn't talking about Todd because she always wrote in her diary at night after he dropped her off."

"And we know he dropped her off at ten," Don added.

"So he says. He could have come back." Jennie stared at the words, committing them to memory.

"Naw, he wouldn't have done that."

"You seem sure."

"I am," Micky said, picking up his drink again. "I was watching TV in my room, and when I went to the bathroom around ten-thirty, I saw Jessica go into her room. I went in to ask her if she wanted to watch a show with me, and she said, 'Not tonight. I have something important to do.'

" 'How's Todd?' I asked, and she said, 'Todd's fine.'

"Then I said, 'You're home kind of early.' She told me Todd had to go to work at five in the morning 'cause he had a charter. She seemed kind of spacy—like something was wrong. Then she told me to go away 'cause she wanted to write." Micky chewed on his lip and glanced toward the window.

With an empathetic look at his friend, Don added, "That was the last time he saw her."

Jennie set the diary back on the table and reached for her cocoa. "Why didn't the sheriff take this earlier? It's evidence."

"Probably because they didn't find it. See, at first I thought they did take it 'cause it wasn't in the place she usually kept it."

"You knew where?"

Micky flushed. "Yeah. Only it wasn't there—I mean, when I went in her room this morning, the diary was lying on her nightstand."

"So you're saying someone took the diary before the police could find it, ripped out the pages, and held on to it until today?"

"Yeah—I guess. M-maybe whoever killed her."

"Why would they put it back?"

Micky shrugged.

"I got an idea." Don wiped his sleeve across his mouth. "What if Jessica's ghost got it from the killer and put it there to help us?"

Jennie gave him a you've-got-to-be-kidding look. "I don't think so. We need to get this to Joe. Micky, did you tell anyone when you saw Jessica come in?"

"Yeah, a couple of deputies, but they didn't believe me 'cause Dad told them Todd was just leaving when he came home. I guess that was around midnight."

"Are you saying your father lied?"

"No! He wouldn't do that. It was dark—maybe he just thought he saw Todd's car."

"Or maybe Todd came back." Jennie picked up the diary—more carefully this time. Any prints that had been there were probably gone by now. She stuck it in a plastic bag to protect it as much as possible, then insisted the boys accompany her to the sheriff's office to give Joe the diary.

———

Joe listened to the story, then gave Micky and Don a stern lecture. By handling the diary, they may have destroyed crucial evidence. "And another thing—" Joe paused to make eye contact with all three of them. "I could arrest you for withholding evidence. No more playing cops and robbers. Is that clear?"

"Yes, sir," Micky and Don echoed.

"That goes for you, too, Jennie."

"I know. Which is why I thought you should know about the diary."

Joe flashed her one of his perfect grins and winked. "I'm glad you did. Now I'd appreciate it if you all went about your business. If you see or hear anything, you tell me. No more trying to figure it out on your own."

Jennie herded the boys to her car again with plans to drop them off. When they emerged from the municipal building, the sun greeted them so warmly that Micky and Don opted to skateboard home. That was fine with Jennie.

Deciding to take advantage of the sun herself, Jennie parked in downtown Bay Village near the seawall. Bay Village had a coastal flavor and was especially beautiful with the mountains to the east and a terrific view of the coastline to the north and south. It sat on a rocky bluff overlooking the ocean. Jennie stood looking at the water for a while. Out beyond the surf she could see four boats—probably loaded with tourists fishing or looking for whales. Speaking of which . . . out beyond the breakers, a whale rose out of the water and spouted. Its spray shot into the air and dissipated.

Jennie loved spotting the whales. She'd seen them from a boat once several years ago. It would be fun to do it again—maybe with Ryan. Jennie turned away and started walking. Maybe not.

Determined not to dwell on her disappointments where Ryan was concerned, Jennie spent the next half hour walking along the seawall, then ducking into the many shops and art galleries along the way. Though Jennie fully intended to leave the investigation of Jessica's death to the authorities, she couldn't turn off her mind. And she couldn't help but notice the political signs in the windows and on doors. *Vote no on gambling. No on Initiative 39.* Nearly every shopkeeper was against it. However, in an empty lot at the end of town, proponents of the bill had erected a huge billboard showing a fabulous multimillion-dollar high-rise. To the left of the billboard was written:

The Bay Village Resort and Casino will bring

- 2,000 new jobs to Lincoln County
- Millions in increased revenue for Bay Village and Oregon schools
- Fun! Fun! Fun! for the entire family

Vote Yes on Initiative 39

In nearly all of the store windows she'd seen something else too—a flyer inviting people to come to the mayor's fundraiser. She'd read something about how the casino actually hurt shopkeepers. The casinos brought in tons more people as advertised, but the traffic was so bad no one wanted to stop at the stores along the way. There were other reasons to oppose gambling, of course. Like the increase in people with gambling addictions.

Maybe she would go to the benefit if Gram didn't mind. She'd meet the artists and some of the other people Jessica hung around with.

Jennie watched a boat come in and wandered down to the docks. Several people disembarked carrying bags of fish they'd caught.

"Looks like you had a good day." Jennie directed her comment to the man still on board.

He had his back to her and was hosing out the fish box. "Had better." He turned around, and Jennie almost backed into the water.

"Oh. Hi. I didn't realize it was you."

Greg Kopelund's puzzled gaze met hers. "Do I know you?"

"Jennie McGrady. Ryan Johnson's friend."

"Oh, right—the junior detective who was going to figure

out how to get my brother out of jail." Greg coiled the hose and jumped onto the wharf.

"You don't need to be sarcastic."

"No, I suppose I don't." He paused and looked her up and down. "You here to ask me questions too? I've already talked to the cops half a dozen times. Guess once more won't hurt."

"No. I just came down to look at the fish. I didn't know it was you. . . ."

"Sure. So what did you want to ask? Do I think Todd is guilty? Of course not. He didn't kill Jessica."

"What time did he get home?"

Greg shrugged. "A little after ten."

"Did he go out again?"

"How should I know? I went to bed."

"Then he could have gone back."

"He says he didn't, and I believe him." Greg smiled, softening his stern features. "I thought you didn't come out here to ask questions."

"You offered to answer them."

"Let me tell you something, Jennie McGrady. My brother's not a killer. If he was, I'd expect the law to come down hard on him. In fact, I'd probably turn him in myself. People should pay for their mistakes. Don't you think?"

"Yes, but—"

"Sorry, Jennie, but I can't stick around. I have an appointment. Annie and I are trying to get some money together for a decent lawyer for Todd. That court-appointed broad couldn't care less. With the mayor pulling out all the stops, I figure we'd better do something."

He boarded the *Linda Sue* and disappeared below deck. Jennie let out a long breath and walked back to the main drag.

Feeling a bit peeved and in dire need of something to drink, Jennie made a sharp right into Charlie Crookston's ice cream parlor. After using the rest room facilities, she went back to the counter and looked over a neatly printed list of available coffee drinks and sodas. The judge must have been working alone, as no one came to wait on her. He sat at a cluttered desk in the back room talking to someone on the phone and slicing open an envelope with a black letter opener.

"I don't care what you have to do. We need to find out what happened to those funds." Charlie's angry look faded when he glanced up at Jennie and mouthed, *Be right there.* Back into the phone he said, "All right. See that you do. We'd better get to the bottom of this and fast. If we let 39 pass it'll be the end of Bay Village as we know it." He paused, then added, "You do that."

Charlie ambled out of the office. "Afternoon, Jennie. What can I get for you today?"

"An Italian soda with the white chocolate macadamia syrup."

"Coming up." After dispensing clear, bubbly soda into a tall glass, Charlie poured in a shot of syrup and another of cream and, after giving it a quick stir, set it on the counter. "Not quite as nosy as your old Gram, are you?"

"What do you mean?" Jennie pulled a five out of her pocket and handed it to him.

He chuckled and gave her back the change. "Helen would have been drilling me about the conversation I just had, and I'd be fixing myself a cup of coffee and telling her all about it."

Putting her change away, Jennie shrugged. "I'm curious, just not as brave."

"In that case, have yourself a seat. I'm busting to tell somebody, and seeing as you're Helen's granddaughter . . ." Charlie poured himself a cup of coffee and joined Jennie at one of the wrought-iron patio tables.

"You been keeping abreast of the big fight we got going on here over the gambling initiative?"

"Sort of." Jennie took a drink of the delicious concoction and would have moaned in ecstasy had someone other than Charlie been sitting there.

"It's an important one," he went on. "You probably heard me tell the sheriff about the missing funds."

Jennie nodded. "Someone stole money from the campaign?"

"Had to fire our campaign manager. Claims he doesn't know what happened." Charlie's face reddened as his voice rose. "Likely story. I'll bet anything he got paid by the enemy camp to siphon the funds over to them. Talk about dirty politics. Now we're left with no money and no one to run the office. Maybe I'll ask your grandmother. She's had experience—and I know we can trust her. Think she'd do it?"

"I don't know—she's pretty busy."

"Aren't we all. Speaking of which—how'd you like a job? I could use some extra help in the shop while I'm trying to straighten up this mess. My daughter usually helps out, but she quit to stay home with the baby." Charlie whipped out photos of his first grandchild.

Twenty minutes later Jennie stood behind the counter making her first latté for her first customer, trying to figure out how she'd let Charlie talk her into it.

"You'll do fine, Jennie." Charlie shrugged into his jacket and reached for the door. "If you have any trouble, call Mindy. Her number's on the yellow Post-it next to the phone."

With that he was gone—headed for the office to find a new campaign manager. Jennie turned back to her customer, Betty Stone, the owner of the used bookstore down the street. "Would you like cream?"

"I suppose I should say no." She patted her ample stomach. "But what the hey. You only live once."

Jennie dropped a spoonful of whipped cream on the hot caramel-colored latté and covered it with a plastic lid. After

Mrs. Stone left, the store was quiet for all of five minutes—long enough for Jennie to call Gram and leave a message on the machine and to read Charlie's personal invitation to the mayor's benefit. Looked like she wouldn't be going after all. One hundred dollars a plate was a little over budget for her.

While she was waiting on the next customer, the phone rang. Before Jennie could break free to answer it, the answering machine clicked on. "Charlie, I need to talk to you right away."

The caller, a woman, hadn't left a name, but Jennie had heard the voice before—Mari Ames. Jennie quickly jotted down the message on the telephone note pad. Another customer came in, then another. The sun was bringing out tourists in droves, and for the next two hours Jennie barely had time to breathe. At five, she pulled off her apron, stepped outside to haul in the two-sided wooden sign, turned the open sign around to read closed, and collapsed on the nearest chair.

She'd expected Charlie back an hour ago and was beginning to worry. Not knowing what to do with the money from the till, Jennie counted it, pulled out the $100 in change and small bills Charlie had told her to leave in the till for the next day, and made out a deposit slip. She put the money—$382.25—and the deposit slip in a bank bag she found lying on the judge's cluttered desk and returned the change to the till. When Charlie still hadn't shown up, Jennie called Mindy.

"Hi, Jennie. How's it going?"

Jennie filled her in, absently picking up the ornate black letter opener. It had a mother-of-pearl inlay—a bit large for a letter opener—and rather lethal-looking with its long and very sharp point. She set it back on the desk. "I guess I did okay, but what do I do with the money?"

"All that's left is to lock up and take the deposit to the bank," Mindy said. "I really appreciate your taking over. Sounds like you have everything under control."

Jennie thanked Mindy and hung up, relieved that she didn't have to wait around for Charlie to come back. She left him a note, collected her backpack, and grabbed her coat. Tucking the deposit bag under one arm, Jennie locked the door and started for her car. A black limousine drove up, blocking her path. The chauffeur, a tall, dark-haired man with a wide forehead and beaklike nose, stepped out and came toward her. Jennie clutched the money tighter, wishing she'd thought to put it out of sight in her backpack.

"Um—I'm sorry, we're closed," she managed to say.

"Where's Judge Crookston?"

"I don't know. He was supposed to—"

"What have you got there?" The man's dark, piercing gaze shifted from her face to the money bag.

"N-nothing," Jennie stammered. She looked wildly from the man to the street. No way was she going to let him get his hands on Charlie's money. Jennie took a step back, then turned and ran.

She made it about two steps.

A firm hand gripped her arm and spun her around. "Not so fast." The man drew a gun from under his jacket. "Get in the car."

# 11

"How many times do I have to tell you I wasn't stealing the money?" Jennie sat in back of the limousine next to the chauffeur with the gun and across from Mayor Ames.

"Then why did you run?" the mayor asked.

"Are you kidding? Have you taken a good look at your bodyguard lately?"

Mayor Ames rubbed his nearly bald head. He looked like a man with a lot of worries. Jennie could understand why. "Hawk, for heaven's sake, put the gun away. She's just a kid."

Hawk did as he was told. "Do you want me to call the sheriff?"

"Not yet. Let's try the judge again." When Hawk picked up the cellular phone, the mayor turned back to Jennie. "I find it hard to believe Judge Crookston would hand over his business to you. Especially since he told me he'd have to meet me here because he couldn't leave the store."

"Charlie hired me so he could take care of some other business. Someone stole the campaign money they'd collected to oppose Initiative 39. I happened to be in the store when he needed someone to take over, that's all."

Hawk set the phone back in its holder. "He isn't answering."

"Call Mindy—his daughter. I just talked to her. She told me to take the money to the bank. She'll verify my story."

Jennie handed him the keys and told them where to find the number. She watched the long-legged Hawk extricate himself from the car. The fear Jennie had felt a few minutes before now settled in an annoying ache in the pit of her stomach. Or maybe it was hunger.

Jennie couldn't remember if she'd eaten since breakfast. She took a deep breath. It would be over soon. They'd hear the truth and let her go. She'd make the deposit at the bank and go back to Gram's. Then she'd call the judge and tell him what he could do with his job.

When she glanced at Mayor Ames, a feeling of sadness mingled with her anger. She opened her mouth to tell him she was sorry about Jessica when Hawk swung open the car door.

"You'd better come inside." Hawk scowled. "I found Charlie."

The dark look on his face told Jennie the news wasn't good. Hawk gripped her arm and pulled her out. Jennie's heart slammed against her chest wall like a sledgehammer.

"What's wrong?" Mayor Ames climbed out of the car behind her, then hurried to catch up.

Hawk was lean, but he had the strength of a weight lifter. He hauled Jennie into the store and pushed her toward the office.

"Take it easy." Jennie plunged in, grabbing the desk to keep from falling flat on her face. Further protests lodged in her throat when she saw the cause of Hawk's fury. Judge Crookston was lying face down on the floor just inside the back door.

"What the . . ." Mayor Ames shoved past her and knelt down at Charlie's side. He turned him over, revealing a bloodstained white shirt.

Ames stood and turned his horror-glazed face toward her. "What have you done?"

"N-nothing, I didn't—" Jennie clutched at the desk's

edge, willing her knees not to buckle. *Stay calm*, she heard a distant voice inside her head say. *Don't panic*. Jennie closed her eyes for an instant, hoping that when she opened them, Judge Crookston's body wouldn't be there and she'd be alone, counting the money, getting ready to close up the shop—or better yet, she'd be drinking her soda, minding her own business. She'd realize the entire afternoon had been a nightmare.

When she opened her eyes, Charlie was still lying on the floor. Hawk had dialed 9–1–1, and Mayor Ames' complexion had turned nearly as chalky white as Charlie's. It was then her brain kicked back in. "I know CPR." Jennie moved away from the desk and forced her legs to make the trek to the motionless man a few feet away. Reaching his side, she dropped to her knees and checked Charlie's airway. She expelled her own breath the moment she felt his against her face and heard his heart beating faintly in her ear. "He's still alive."

"Are you sure?" The mayor hunkered down beside her. "He looks so—"

Jennie cut him off and asked Hawk to hand her a towel from a shelf of linens behind him. She could hear the welcome sound of sirens as she unbuttoned the judge's shirt. He had been stabbed. The small stab wound was no longer bleeding, but Jennie pressed the cloth to it anyway, then backed away when the EMTs from the nearby fire station charged in and took over. Joe Adams and a deputy arrived seconds later to assist, and within five minutes Charlie Crookston was on his way to the hospital.

"Care to explain what happened here?" Joe took a note pad and pen out of his breast pocket.

Jennie, Hawk, and the mayor all started talking at once.

"Whoa. Hold on." Joe held up his hand to silence them. "One at a time. Jennie, suppose you start."

Jennie explained how she'd gone for a walk and ended up with a job and being detained by the mayor and Hawk. "All

I know is that Judge Crookston wasn't here when I left. He must have come in the back after I locked up. Or someone brought him in." She looked up and cringed at the hard, beady-eyed gaze Hawk leveled at her. It was a good nickname for him. At any moment she expected him to swoop down on her. His long, bony fingers gripped the back of the judge's wooden chair like talons. It seemed odd the mayor would hang around with a man like that.

"What do you mean—someone brought him in?" Joe asked, dragging Jennie's mind back to Charlie.

Jennie nodded toward the back door. "There's not much blood on the floor—at least not that I could see. 'Course, the wound isn't very big. And I don't see a weapon either. Whoever stabbed the judge must have done it somewhere else. Maybe outside or—"

Almost as if on cue, the deputy came out of the office where he'd been going over the room looking for evidence. "Found the weapon." He held up a clear plastic baggy.

Jennie sucked in a wild breath. The officer was holding the ornate ebony and mother-of-pearl letter opener she'd played with not more than a half hour ago.

"It's about the right size," Joe said. "I'll lay odds Charlie's blood is all over it. Did you dust it for prints?"

The deputy nodded. "Got a couple real clear ones— small—possibly a woman's."

"I . . . they might be mine." Jennie hardly recognized her strained, high-pitched voice. She cleared her throat and tried again. "It was on his desk earlier. I picked it up when I was on the phone."

Joe didn't seem surprised or angry. He simply nodded, made a notation on his pad, and moved back to the questions he'd been asking before. It didn't take long to verify that Jennie had indeed been working for the judge and that Mayor Ames and Hawk had been operating under a false assumption. Joe let Jennie go, promising to let her know as soon as he learned anything about Charlie's condition.

"You'll be in town for a while, won't you, Jennie?"

"Sure—till the end of next week."

Jennie's hands were shaking when she inserted the key into the door to unlock her car. Glancing around to make sure she wasn't being followed, she checked the backseat, then climbed in. For good measure she locked herself in and headed for the bank. It had closed at six, so Jennie pulled in close to the drive-through and dropped the bag in the night deposit slot.

"Relax," she told herself. "There's no one following you." Jennie started to pull out of the bank parking lot, then stopped when she noticed a white Toyota whiz by. Camilla's car. And Ryan was driving. Ryan either hadn't seen her or had chosen not to acknowledge her. Jennie suspected the latter. Fine.

Ignoring the lump in her throat and the even bigger one in her stomach, Jennie turned in the opposite direction and headed back to Gram's. At least there everything would be normal.

Jennie pulled into Orcas Drive just as J.B., Gram, and Nick were pulling out. She moved over to the side and rolled down the window. "Where are you headed?"

"To dinner. We came back from town earlier than we expected and hoped you'd be here," Gram said. "Thought we'd stop at Charlie's to see if we could find you."

"Why don't you park your car, lass, and come join us?" J.B. suggested. "We'll be going to your gram's favorite restaurant to catch the sunset."

"Sounds great. Would you mind waiting while I change? I feel pretty grungy." They agreed and a half hour later they piled into J.B.'s Cadillac. Nick scooted close and snuggled against her.

"We got a postcard from Mom and Dad!" he announced. "They shoulda took us with them."

Jennie hugged him and buckled herself, then him in. "I don't think so. Kids don't usually go along on honeymoons."

"They could. Mama said she wished we were there and next time they'll bring us along."

Jennie wrapped an arm around him and laughed. "I wish they would have taken us too." She didn't add that at the moment she'd rather be anywhere else but in the same state as Ryan Johnson.

Listening to Nick and J.B. talk about their outing, Jennie began to relax. She needed to tell Gram and J.B. about Charlie, but that could wait until later—when Nick had gone to bed.

The evening promised to be a good one. Jennie snuggled back against the plush leather seat and switched between making faces at Nick and talking with Gram and J.B. about Hawaii. They'd both been there. She hadn't. But she had been in the Caribbean and could imagine the tropical breezes and palm trees.

She wondered how Mom and Dad were getting along. Jennie told herself not to worry. They loved each other and had vowed to work things out. Still, the old concerns about their differences and arguments crept through the back of her mind.

The sun, still a glowing red ball, hung in the western sky when they pulled into the parking lot at The Tidal Waves. Jennie climbed out of the car and waited for Nick to join her. He raced to the door and strained to open it. J.B. chuckled and gave him a hand.

Jennie shut the car door and straightened. Her heart dropped like a runaway elevator and hit bottom. They'd pulled in right next to Camilla's car.

"Darling, are you all right?" Gram asked.

Jennie nodded. "Ryan's here with Camilla."

"Oh, dear." Gram wrapped an arm around Jennie's

shoulders. "Do you want to leave? We can go somewhere else."

"No," Jennie answered quickly. "It's okay." It wasn't, of course, but Jennie refused to run away. Sooner or later she'd have to face him—might as well be now. The town was too small to dodge him and Camilla forever.

Jennie straightened and walked into the restaurant with her head high.

They waited a few minutes for the busboy to clear a table by the window, then followed the hostess down the steps. The restaurant was small, built on two levels, and offered an unobstructed view of Depoe Bay and the ocean beyond. For a few wonderful moments, Jennie thought perhaps she'd been mistaken about Camilla's car. It wasn't until she sat down that she caught sight of Ryan and his date. They were seated on the upper level at the opposite end of the restaurant. Camilla leaned forward and apparently said something funny. Ryan laughed. Jennie tried to ignore the jealousy gnawing at her stomach, choosing instead to call it hunger.

"I'm starved," she said aloud, lifting the menu high enough to cover her view of the happy couple.

She ordered halibut fish and chips with a shrimp salad, doubting she'd be able to eat a bite, then focused on the sunset as it turned the bay into a magical array of color. The next time she looked up, Camilla and Ryan were gone. Jennie doubted Ryan had even seen them. Or if he had, he'd chosen to ignore her.

Relief poured out in a long sigh. Seeing them together had been hurtful but not impossible. When her meal came, Jennie downed her food, then finished off with half of Nick's decadent brownie a la mode.

J.B. paid the bill, and they left. The day was nearly over, and Jennie could hardly wait until bedtime. In fact, as they turned off the main road, heading for home, she seriously considered going to her room and hiding out with a good book. She might have, too, if Ryan hadn't come over the minute they pulled into the driveway.

"What does he want?" she muttered under her breath.

"Don't you like Ryan anymore?" Nick asked.

Jennie didn't know how to answer. Of course she liked him. She told Nick as much. "I'm kind of upset with him right now because he likes someone else."

"But you're still friends, right? My teacher says that when friends get other friends then that's good 'cause you can have more friends 'cause maybe their friends can be yours."

*Some friend.* "It's hard to explain, Nick." Jennie climbed out of the car, eager to escape.

After greeting Gram, J.B., and Nick, Ryan pulled Jennie aside. "We have to talk."

Jennie stuffed her hands in her jacket pockets and waited until the others had gone inside. "I'm not sure we have anything to talk about."

"Come on, McGrady. Knock it off. I took Camilla to dinner to talk to her about Todd and Jessica—that's all. You could have come."

"I did, but you were having so much fun I didn't want to disturb you." Jennie cringed at the ugly sarcasm in her voice.

"You were at the restaurant?"

"Yes, and I saw the way you were *talking* to her."

"What's that supposed to mean?"

"Nothing."

"You're jealous." Ryan smiled when he said it.

"I'm not." Jennie turned her face away from him. "I couldn't care less."

"Well, if you're not jealous and you don't care, then there's no problem." Ryan extended his hand to her, palm up. "Let's go for a walk."

Jennie hesitated. She'd always had trouble resisting those eyes. Now was no exception. She took his hand and walked with him down Orcas Lane.

Ryan didn't speak again until they reached the main road and cut back down a side road that would eventually lead them around a loop through one of Bay Village's wealthier neighborhoods and past the Ames house.

Jennie liked the silence. Her thoughts drifted between calling herself names for being so forgiving and thinking how perfect her hand fit into Ryan's and how right it felt to be walking beside him.

"I heard you went to see Todd today." Ryan held firm to her hand when she started to withdraw it.

"So?"

"So, what did you talk about?"

"Basically he told me he didn't do it."

"And you called him a liar." Ryan's hair turned the color of spun gold as they passed under a streetlight.

"He tell you that?"

"Yeah. He told me something else too, Jennie. You were right, Jennie. Todd lied—to me and to all of us. It looks like he may have killed Jessica after all."

# 12

"Oh no . . ." Jennie started to tell him about the political overtones of the case and the possibility that Todd had been set up, but Ryan didn't give her the opportunity.

"Joe questioned him about the ring, and he started crying. He admitted that Jessica really had broken up with him. She tried to give him back the ring, but he wouldn't take it so she set it on the wall and went inside. He claims he doesn't know how it got down on the rocks."

"What made him decide to tell the truth—that is, if he's telling the truth?"

"You . . . the ring." Ryan stopped and drew her into the circle of his arms.

Jennie leaned back. "Did he confess to pushing her over the cliff?"

"You seem surprised." He dropped his arms to his side. "Isn't that what you were thinking all along?"

"No—I mean, yes, but—" Jennie shook her head. After what had happened with Charlie, Jennie felt certain Todd must be innocent, but maybe the two cases were unrelated. Maybe Jessica's death had nothing to do with the attack on Charlie. Still, they hung together in Jennie's mind like matching socks, both with holes big enough to poke a fist through. And after what Joe had said about organized crime . . . "Did Todd tell you he killed Jessica?" she asked again.

"Not exactly. I left after he told me about the argument."

"So you're just assuming he did it."

"Who else would have done it, Jennie?" He raked a hand through his hair. "I don't get it. All this time I'm saying Todd's innocent, and you don't think so. Now I'm agreeing that I think he's probably guilty, and you sound like you think he isn't. What gives?"

"I wish I knew." Jennie told him about her run-in with the mayor and Hawk—and about Charlie. "I could be way wrong, but I have a strong hunch Jessica's murder, the attack on Charlie, and the stolen money are all related."

"Seems to me Joe is right. We're better off staying as far away from the case as possible. What you just described sounds like one of those old gangster movies. You know, where some big lug gets word from his boss to knock off somebody's relative to make sure they follow the *rules*." Ryan emphasized the last word.

"I was thinking the same thing. Hawk could be cast in the movie. He's scary. I guess that's a good thing to have in a bodyguard." Jennie paused for a moment, letting her new thoughts jell. "Ryan, this Hawk guy, I don't think I've ever seen him around before. Come to think of it, I don't remember the mayor riding around in a limo before either. And why would he need a bodyguard . . . unless someone was threatening him?"

"I suppose that's a possibility. I can understand him wanting a bodyguard, coming out against the gambling initiative like he has. As for the limo—the mayor likes to use one when he's going to some big party or fund-raiser, so that's not unusual. I guess some people are impressed by it. My folks say it's a waste of taxpayers' money."

"Hmm. A lot to think about." Jennie tipped her head back, letting the wind and mist off the ocean hit her full in the face.

As they walked past Jessica's place, Jennie's thoughts

switched from the mayor to his daughter. The house was dark except for a large yard light and another light over the porch. The porch led directly into the kitchen. Like so many houses, Gram's included, the back of the house faced the street. The front faced the ocean to take advantage of the view. Jennie had the strongest urge to turn into the driveway. Her mind drifted back to Jessica's diary and the missing pages. If she could get inside . . . maybe—

"Where are you going?" Ryan pulled her back beside him.

"I—" Jennie stopped. Without realizing it, she'd turned into the driveway. "Um—I don't know." She shivered. "Never mind, it's just too weird."

Jennie glanced back at the house. A light went on in one of the rooms upstairs. Whatever had compelled her was gone now. She hooked her arm around Ryan's elbow and started toward home.

"Jennie," Ryan began after they'd gone a few steps. "You were right about Camilla."

"What do you mean?"

"You said she thought of me as more than a friend."

"I'm not sure I want to hear this." Jennie held her breath.

"I think you need to. See, I should have listened to you. By going out to dinner with her I hurt you both. I didn't mean to." He squeezed Jennie's hand. "I got too focused on trying to prove Todd innocent. Anyway, I straightened Camilla out. Told her I didn't see her as anything more than a friend."

Jennie swallowed. "So now you have to straighten me out too, huh?"

"Yep—that's my plan." He stopped under a streetlamp and turned to face her. He clasped both hands behind her head, trapping her and forcing her to meet his eyes. "I told Camilla I already had a girlfriend—someone I care a lot about."

"Oh." Jennie released a puff of breath that turned white

when it hit the cold air. Butterflies flittered in chaotic movements when Ryan kissed her.

When he raised his head an instant later, Jennie smiled. "I take it that means we're more than friends."

He chuckled and slung an arm over her shoulder. "You could say that."

———

The next morning during a French toast and sausage breakfast, Joe came by.

Gram insisted he stay for breakfast and poured him a cup of coffee. "How's poor Charlie this morning?"

"Better." Joe pulled out the empty chair next to Jennie and sat down. "He's a lucky man. That letter opener missed his heart by about a quarter of an inch." Joe took a sip of coffee and let his dark brown gaze settle on Jennie. "I know it was a nuisance for you, Jennie, having the mayor and Hawk think you were stealing that money, but it was a blessing in disguise. If you hadn't gone back into the office, old Charlie would have died."

"Glad I could help."

Joe gave her a crooked grin. "Looks like he'll be going home in a day or two."

"Any idea who might have wanted to do him in?" J.B. asked.

"Not yet. The only good prints we found on the weapon are Jennie's." He buttered his French toast and reached for the syrup.

"You don't think Jennie—" J.B. scowled.

"Not at all." Joe sliced off a square of French toast and popped it into his mouth. After an expectant moment, he added, "Charlie can't identify his assailant but says he got him from behind. All he remembers is getting a thump on the head and seeing stars. He was at the campaign office going through some files at the time. For whatever reason, the attacker took him back to the office and stuck him with his own letter opener."

"Maybe he wanted to make it look like a break-in," Gram said.

"Looks that way. They apparently waited until Jennie left, then went in the back door, dumped the body, and took off."

"Any suspects?" J.B. asked, finishing off his sausage.

"Trevor Smith. He's the campaign manager Charlie fired. Claims he had nothing to do with the missing money or the attack on the judge." Joe shifted his gaze to Gram, then Jennie, then back to J.B. "It's looking more and more like the pro-gambling constituents have taken to playing dirty. Then again, it might not have anything to do with the campaign— being a judge, he's stepped on a lot of toes."

After finishing his breakfast and coffee, Joe started to leave. Jennie followed him out, wanting to ask about Mayor Ames and his bodyguard. The more she thought about it, the more puzzled she became. Who was Hawk, and why was he driving the mayor around in a limo? Jennie asked but didn't get the response she'd hoped for.

"Why the questions, Jennie?" Joe asked. "I thought I told you to stay out of the investigation."

"Just curious. I think I have a right to know who he is. He did hold me at gunpoint."

"Well, you can put your suspicions aside. Hawk's not nearly as fierce as he looks. His uncle runs the casino in Siletz Bay."

"How come I've never seen him around before?"

Joe shrugged and opened his car door. "He hasn't worked for the mayor all that long."

Jennie waited until he'd gotten into his car and rolled down the window, then asked, "You said his uncle runs the casino. Does that mean he wants the gambling bill to pass?"

"Not necessarily. Why do you ask?"

"If he's for it, don't you find it strange that he'd be working for the mayor?"

Joe shook his head and picked up his radio receiver in response to a call. "On my way." He started the engine and shifted into reverse. "I'm not sure where you're going with this, Jennie, but I suggest you find something else to occupy your time. In the meantime, I'd better go. The mayor's carrying out his campaign promise to be tough on crime. Problem is, he keeps passing the ball to me."

Jennie watched him drive away, then ran back into the house.

It wasn't much, but the oddity of the mayor's choice of chauffeur/bodyguard set off her sense of curiosity. So did the fact that the mayor and Hawk just happened to be in the area when Charlie was hurt, and Hawk just happened to find him. Okay, so Joe had told her not to get involved in Jessica's murder investigation, but he hadn't said anything about Charlie or the gambling initiative or the stolen money. Maybe she could do some digging—discreetly, of course. Joe had suggested she find something else to occupy her time.

"Jennie! Telephone," Gram called from the kitchen.

"Who is it?" Jennie hurried through the entry and took the phone from Gram's extended hand.

"It's Charlie."

"Hi, Jennie," Charlie greeted. "I heard about the trouble you had with the mayor and his driver. Sorry you had to go through all that."

"It was worth the trouble to have found you. How are you feeling?"

"Not bad, considering. Listen, I know it's a lot to ask, but I'd sure appreciate it if you could keep working at the shop until I can get out of here. Your gram's agreed to help with the campaign."

*No way,* she started to say but couldn't. "Sure. I guess."

"That's great. Somehow I knew I could count on you two. Do you still have the keys?"

"Yeah." Hawk had given them back to her the night before.

Jennie didn't share Charlie's enthusiasm. "Um, Judge Crookston, could I ask you something?"

"Fire away."

"You know the mayor pretty well, don't you?"

"Yep. Forrest and I go way back."

"Have you met his bodyguard—a guy named Hawk?"

"Hawk—" He hesitated. "Can't say as I have. Why do you ask?"

"Just curious. I guess he must be new."

After receiving some last-minute instructions about the shop, Charlie wished her luck and reminded her to call Mindy if she needed help. Jennie returned the phone to its base.

"What's wrong, darling?" Gram slid an arm around Jennie's shoulder. "If you're that upset about working at the shop, we can call Charlie back. I'm sure he can find someone. . . ."

"No, it isn't that. I think Judge Crookston just lied to me."

# 13

Gram raised an eyebrow. "Are you certain? I've known Charlie a long time, Jennie, and I've never known him to be dishonest."

"Charlie said he didn't know Hawk. But Hawk knew Charlie. At least well enough to recognize him yesterday. Hawk went into the office to call Mindy. Then he came out and said he found Charlie. It wasn't like 'I think I found him.' He knew."

"I'm not certain that means anything. I would imagine a lot of people know Charlie that he wouldn't recognize. But it is an interesting point. Perhaps I could stop by the hospital and have a little chat with him on my way to the campaign office today."

"That'd be great." Jennie glanced around. "What happened to Nick and J.B.?"

"They've taken Bernie for a walk."

"Oh." She was supposed be caring for Nick, but J.B. seemed to be doing everything. "Do you think it's a good idea if we both work? I mean—what about Nick?"

"J.B. said he'd be happy to take care of Nick while we're gone. In case you haven't noticed, those two are inseparable."

Jennie smiled. "I've noticed. Are you sure he can manage? I mean, he's not used to having kids around."

"Oh, I think they'll manage just fine."

———

At nine-thirty, Jennie inserted the key into the lock, pushed open the door to Charlie's ice cream shop, and turned on the lights. The first thing she did was close the door to the office so she wouldn't have to think about coming in and seeing Charlie there with a hole in his chest.

Maybe scooping ice cream, cream-cheesing bagels, and making lattés was a good thing. Relishing in the sunshine that streamed through the windows, Jennie made coffee and set out all the essential tools and the recipes for all the coffee drinks and various cream-cheese mixtures, then cleaned the tables with a special bleach solution as Charlie had instructed. Mindy had replenished the cream cheeses the day before so she wouldn't have to make up any new. At least not right away.

At nine-forty-five, she opened the door and accepted the load of bagels that, according to the driver, had been baked fresh in Lincoln City that morning.

At ten, she set out the advertising board, turned the sign from closed to open, and went behind the counter. The morning sped by as Jennie served one customer after another—a steady stream, but not unmanageable. Noontime, though, brought dozens, and Jennie worked harder at staying calm than at serving customers. When Ryan came in to see how she was doing, she put him to work taking orders and delivering them to the tables. He stayed until two, when business settled back down again.

"I nearly forgot what I came in to tell you." Ryan slipped on his jacket. "Gram said we should go with her to the benefit at the mayor's house."

"We're going? It's kind of spendy, isn't it?"

"Too rich for me, that's for sure, but since she's the new campaign manager, we all get to go free. It should be fun."

"Yeah. Um—what are we supposed to wear?" Jennie hoped it would be casual since she hadn't brought much other than jeans and tops.

He shrugged. "Something dressy. Gram said she'd get you something." A car pulled up in front of the store, and two women got out. Ryan left, probably to avoid being put back to work.

———

When Jennie closed up shop for the day, she had no black limo waiting for her, nor was she accosted making her run to the bank to deposit the money. The afternoon had been just busy enough to keep her from being bored or from thinking too much about Charlie—and Jessica.

Now, as she made her way home, Jennie's mind drifted back to the cliff in front of Forrest and Mari Ames' home and back to the girl who'd experienced a tragic death there. Jessica had broken up with Todd, and he'd lied about it. He denied killing her though, and after what had happened to Charlie, Jennie tended to believe him.

"What did Charlie and Jessica have in common?" she asked her reflection in the rear view mirror. The answer came back like it had before—the fight against gambling in Bay Village. Still, it seemed farfetched to think Jessica would be involved enough to warrant being murdered unless—Jennie went back to an old premise—Jessica knew something or was simply used as a means to get to the mayor.

Jennie had read books and seen movies where people who were into gambling would at times do terrible things to get their way. Despite Joe's reassurance that Hawk was not a threat, Jennie puzzled about him working for the mayor. Unless the mayor was up to something. Pulling into the drive, Jennie sighed. Things were getting more complicated by the minute. Maybe she'd learn something tonight at the benefit.

The house seemed empty when she first stepped inside. "Gram? Are you home?"

"Upstairs."

Jennie took the stairs two at a time. Gram had half the clothes out of her closet and lying on the bed.

"What are you doing?"

"Trying to find something suitable to wear tonight—for both of us."

"Is it formal?"

"Suit-and-tie. You'll need something other than jeans."

"I don't need to go."

"Of course you do. You'll enjoy it."

"Who'll take care of Nick?"

"J.B." Gram grinned. "Who else? He called a bit ago to tell me they'd gone back to the aquarium. Nick's quite taken by the whale. Claims Keiko smiles and waves at him."

"That wouldn't surprise me. Whales and dolphins do some pretty unique things." Jennie flopped on a clear spot of bed. "Did you find out about Hawk?"

"No, Jennie, I'm sorry. No one I talked with today knew much about him. Only that Forrest hired him after Jessica's death. Perhaps we can find out more at the benefit tonight."

"My thoughts exactly."

Gram reached into the back of her closet and pulled out a magenta dress with a V neck and a white jacket. "This one should fit you. I'm afraid I don't have many clothes in your size." Although Jennie and Gram were similar in height, Gram was a size or two larger.

It wasn't exactly a style Jennie would have chosen. Too matronly. But Jennie didn't really care. As long as it fit—which it did. She borrowed a pair of low-heeled shoes and nylons.

Gram chose a loose-fitting gauzy white dress with gold chains at the neck. She looked artistic and beautiful.

Jennie, Ryan, and Gram drove up to the door of the mayor's home at seven sharp. A valet took the keys from Gram when she stepped out. Ryan escorted both women inside. He looked gorgeous in his rented tux. For a moment Jennie wished she'd let Gram take her into Lincoln City to pick up a new dress. But logic prevailed. The last thing she needed was another fancy dress. The one she had gotten for her cruise was hanging in her closet next to a bridesmaid dress she'd probably never wear again.

Sucking in a determined breath, Jennie stepped inside. Clothes weren't that important to her—on the other hand, she didn't want to seem out of place. She needn't have worried. While most of the men wore tuxes, the women were dressed in a variety of suits and dresses from casual to sequined evening wear.

"Want something to drink?" Ryan eyed the tables at the far end of the formal dining room.

"Sure."

He wandered over to a table set up with punch and coffee and dipped a silver ladle into a large crystal bowl. There must have been a hundred food items set out on the lavishly decorated tables.

Annie, dressed in a white tunic and chef hat, brought in a bowl of something and set it on the table.

"Hi." Jennie approached Annie warily. It seemed strange to see Todd's cousin at an event put on by the mayor and his wife—especially with the mayor being so adamant about Todd's guilt.

When Jennie asked about it, Annie gave her a wry smile.

"I suspect it's because Mayor Ames is a fair man. He knows I'm not responsible for what Todd did—or may have done. Besides, he's crazy about my cooking."

"What about you? Doesn't it bother you to work for

someone who thinks Todd killed their daughter?"

Annie bit into her lower lip. "It's money."

Mayor Ames approached, then, bringing an end to Jennie's questions.

"You've done it again, Annie. Everything looks great." Mayor Ames lifted the lid on one of the hot items. Steam rose to his face. He sniffed deeply. "Mind if I sample?"

Annie laughed. "Not from this one. I fixed you a plate in the kitchen so you wouldn't be getting into my artwork before it's ready."

Mayor Ames followed Annie into the other room like a puppy begging for table scraps.

"What are you laughing at?" Ryan handed her a goblet of pink punch.

"The mayor. He went into the kitchen with Annie to sample the food."

"That's funny?"

"Never mind." Jennie's smile faded as she wondered what had happened to Hawk. If he really was a bodyguard, wouldn't he be hanging around? Anything could happen at a party like this. Jennie made a mental note to check later.

Ryan glanced around. "Hey, there's a guy with an hors d'oeuvres tray. You hungry?"

"Not yet. You go ahead. I want to look around."

"I'll catch up to you later." Ryan wandered off again.

Jennie felt almost relieved to be on her own. Like before, something about the house or its former occupant seemed to be nagging at her. She needed to think and had the feeling she ought to be taking notes.

Only a handful of people had come on time. Gram was talking to Mari Ames and some people Jennie didn't recognize. Jennie moved away from the entry into the living room, where the artists were showing their work. The artists who'd donated pieces to the show—and who'd worked with Jessica.

Several new bronze pieces sat on the living room floor.

One of them drew Jennie forward. Eric had created a thirty-six-inch bronze of Jessica in ballet slippers and a delicate swirling satin dress, lifting her kitten high above her head. Exquisite was the only word Jennie could come up with to describe it. The features of the face looked as though Jessica herself had somehow been miniaturized and dipped in the liquid metal.

"You like it." A man in his thirties ambled up beside her. "I can tell."

"It's beautiful." Jennie's gaze met his gray-green one. "You're the artist, aren't you?"

"Am I that obvious?" Before she could answer, he held out a hand. "Eric Meyers."

Jennie introduced herself and shook his hand before turning back to the bronze. "How do you make them so lifelike?"

"I've had a lot of practice. He glanced admiringly at the piece, then said, "I should tell you—this one isn't for sale. I made it as a gift to Mari and Forrest."

"Jessica took classes from you, didn't she?"

Eric studied her for a moment. His eyes grayed. "Yes. Unfortunately she died before she could finish her first project. She'd hoped to give this to her parents."

"Jessica did this?"

"Um—no, actually. She drew it but never quite got the hang of sculpting it."

"Did you know Jessica well?"

"Well enough. Mari is a good friend. Jessica came more to please her mother than herself. I don't think she was particularly interested in bronze work—seemed more suited to clay."

"Eric!" Gram came up to them. "Good to see you again. Eric is one of my favorite artists, Jennie. I've had my eye on his mermaids for a long time."

"Perhaps now would be a good time to purchase a piece," Eric said. "I brought one of my favorites. You can own your sculpture and help keep gambling out of Bay Village with only one check."

Gram laughed. "Such a bargain."

Jennie left them to work out the details of what could prove to be a profitable evening for Eric and a costly one for Gram. Needing to find a rest room, Jennie made her way down the hallway. The rest room was the first door to the left, but voices coming from the room to the right stopped her.

"I told you I had everything under control," a man's raspy voice said.

"Control!" The second, more menacing voice sounded in danger of losing it. "Crookston came *this* close to finding out. Need I remind you what that would do to our operation?"

"Not to mention *your* reputation." He paused. "Don't worry. Everything is set. I can assure you there won't be any slipups."

Jennie moved closer to the door and grasped the knob. If she could open it a crack, she might be able to see. The doorknob turned in her hand. Someone was coming out.

# 14

Jennie's heart skittered like a frightened rabbit. She slipped into the bathroom across the hall. Holding the door partway open, she peeked through the narrow slit, trying to see who the voices belonged to. Because of the angle, Jennie couldn't see them but suspected one of those voices must belong to the mayor. Or someone who knew his house. If Jennie remembered right from her previous visit—that room was Mayor Ames' office.

After using the facilities, Jennie paused at the room the two men had come out of and turned the knob—it was locked. She hurried back to the party. Maybe if she listened to the voices of some of the guests, she'd be able to tell whom she'd overheard. The information could lead to Charlie's attacker—and perhaps even to Jessica's killer.

Jennie spotted Mayor Ames walking toward the buffet table. She glanced around at the guests. There were about twenty or so now and more arriving every few minutes. Silver-haired and stately, Senator Baker stood near the entry beside his wife—a petite woman who barely came up to his shoulder. His eyes narrowed when he glanced in the mayor's direction.

Jennie sensed hostility in the way he crossed the room— like a lion stalking its prey. Mayor Ames greeted the senator with a smile, then motioned for him to follow. Which he did, down the hall and into the office.

Jennie waited until the door closed, then trailed after them—or she would have if someone hadn't grabbed her arm.

"Where do you think you're going?" Hawk's dark eyes peered down at her, holding her in place. "And don't tell me you're headed for the bathroom because you just came from there."

"I . . . I just wanted to look around."

"Don't you mean snoop? What the senator and Mayor Ames are discussing is no concern of yours. Now I suggest you run along. I understand the food is great, and I think there's a young man looking for you."

Hawk released her and blocked the hallway. Had he been the one in the mayor's office earlier? Maybe she'd been right about Hawk and the mayor being involved in Charlie's near-death experience.

Jennie found Ryan talking to Annie at the buffet table.

"I didn't realize you were such a good cook." Ryan popped a tiny meatball coated in some kind of sauce into his mouth.

"Been cooking for a long time. After my father's accident I had to learn to satisfy all the hungry men in my family. Todd and Greg still eat half their meals at my house."

"Well, anytime you need a guinea pig to sample new stuff, I'll volunteer."

"I just might take you up on that, but only if you'll take the job. I'm desperate for an assistant."

"Sorry, but I'm already taken. I'll be working for Greg for the next couple months."

"Too bad. If you change your mind, I have better benefits."

"When did you decide to work for Greg?" Jennie asked.

"Yesterday."

Annie lifted the lid from a huge stainless-steel pot and

dipped in a ladle, lifting up a tomato broth and a variety of shellfish.

"Is that cioppino?" The seafood soup was one of Jennie's favorites.

"Mmm—my second batch. Want a sample?" At Jennie's enthusiastic nod, Annie scooped some into a bowl and handed it to her.

"Thanks."

Ryan caught Jennie's gaze and grinned. "Want to walk out to the gazebo with me?"

Jennie hesitated. What she really wanted to do was ask questions of some of the guests. One glance back told her the predator was still watching. She picked up a plate, set the cioppino on it, gathered a few other delicacies, then followed Ryan outside.

"Where'd you disappear to anyway?" Ryan asked as he sat on the white bench inside the gazebo.

She told him about the discussion she'd overheard and how Hawk had stopped her from following Senator Baker and Mayor Ames. "They're up to something, Ryan. Whatever it is, Charlie got too close and posed a danger, so they tried to kill him."

"If you're suggesting Mayor Ames or Senator Baker had anything to do with the attack on Charlie, you can forget it. They're all close friends. On the other hand, maybe they're all being threatened."

Jennie speared a spiced prawn. "I don't suppose you saw who came out of the mayor's office a few minutes ago, did you?"

"I saw him with several people." Ryan scanned the crowd that had gathered on the lawn. "There, next to Mrs. Ames. He might be the one. I noticed him talking to the mayor earlier."

Jennie swung around to look. The man, obviously a Native American, had a wide, chiseled face and a long dark braid. Mrs. Ames looked as though she were about to cry, then abruptly walked away. The man shook his head and watched Mrs. Ames for a moment before turning back into the house.

"I'm going to talk to him." Jennie kept her gaze riveted on the stranger's broad back.

"You may want to wait."

Eric Meyers stepped on a platform and spoke into a microphone. "Everyone, I'd like your attention, please." His voice rose above the din, effectively stilling the numerous conversations. "As you know, Jessica Ames had a deep appreciation of the arts—as do her parents, Forrest and Mari Ames. She was also a strong advocate for keeping gambling out of Bay Village. For that reason, Mayor Ames and Mari have dedicated this benefit to her."

Jennie glanced back to where she'd last seen the Native American. He was gone. Making a mental note to catch him later, she and Ryan moved with the others closer to the podium.

Eric went on and on, making a big deal out of donating his gift to the Ameses, then introduced two other artists who'd also brought gifts. While each artist talked, Jennie wondered what kind of role they had played in Jessica's life and how well they knew her.

It seemed odd to Jennie that all three of the artists would have a work either made or begun by Jessica to present. It was a farfetched idea, but Jennie went with it nonetheless. Often in a murder case, the least likely suspect ended up being the killer. Could one of these artists have had anything to do with Jessica's death?

*Naw.* She shook her head. It didn't fit. What would their motives be? They all seemed genuinely saddened by Jessica's passing. Better to listen for clues into Jessica's character than get hung up with more suspicions.

Dana Coons had become famous for her portraits of

children and presented the Ameses with a portrait of Jessica. The painting was one of Jessica in a white gauzy dress, sitting on a rock with the water lapping at her feet.

Nicole Hemingway, the next artist to speak, was a potter. Nicole presented Jessica's parents with a clay figure Jessica herself had made only days before her death. The crude, hand-built piece had been raku fired. A shiny copper cape hung lifelessly on a figure with no head. The cape opened halfway down to reveal a child's face. Lack of glaze on the face made it a haunting shade of charcoal gray.

When they'd finished the presentations, Eric reminded them why they'd come. "On each piece you'll find an opening bid. As this is a silent auction, you'll want to write down the amount you're willing to pay. Someone may outbid you during the course of the evening. Remember, the one with the last bid will be the new owner."

The murmuring crowd dispersed. Many made their way into the house to look over the artwork and make their bids.

Mari Ames again thanked the artists, then moved toward her husband. "Forrest, I'm sorry—" She leaned against him and rubbed her head. "All this excitement has brought on another headache. I hope you don't mind taking over for me while I rest for a few minutes."

"Certainly, sweetheart—would you like me to walk you up?"

"No, stay with our guests."

Mrs. Ames went inside. After watching his wife for a long moment, the mayor turned back to the artists.

The gifts had been placed on a black velvet-covered table near the podium, and Jennie and Ryan wandered over to take a closer look. Only one had actually been done by Jessica alone. Jennie found the child's face eerie and wondered if the work might have some special meaning. Maybe it did. The piece was draped in shiny colors, while inside—

"Ryan, that's it," Jennie said. "What Jessica's saying is

that her life is glossy and warm on the outside, but it's drab—or colorless, cool—or maybe even dark on the inside. She wasn't what people thought. Or maybe the cape represents her father—or mother—an authority figure. The key is that the outside is a facade. She's insignificant, but she can see the world outside. She can see the truth."

Ryan looked at her as though she'd turned into a space alien while she continued. "I think it's her true self trying to come out. Of course, if you consider what happened to the clay—it's been through fire. Part came out beautiful—the rest charred and dull."

Jennie stared at the piece, hoping it might have an answer as to why someone wanted Jessica dead. Nothing more came. Working on her hunch that all was not as it seemed in the Ames family, Jennie announced to Ryan her plans to talk to the mayor, who had gone through the buffet again and was walking toward the stone wall. Jennie glanced around and, seeing no sign of Hawk, followed Mayor Ames across the lawn.

"Hello, Jennie," he said as she approached. "I hope you've recovered from our little misunderstanding yesterday."

"I'm glad it happened, otherwise Charlie might not have been found in time."

"Yes. That's a good way to look at it. Things happen for a reason." Mayor Ames' gaze drifted out to sea. He remained silent for several seconds, then said, "She fell to her death on these rocks. It's a miracle she wasn't washed away. I was the first to find her, you know."

"That must have been really hard for you."

"I've been trying to find a reason. Can't think of any. Every day I ask God why. Why did my baby girl have to die? Why couldn't it have been me?" He looked at Jennie. A film of tears covered his pale blue eyes.

Jennie swallowed back the lump of empathy in her throat. "I don't know."

"No, of course you don't. I wish I'd come back earlier that night—wish I'd never gone into town." He hauled in a deep breath and closed his eyes. Perspiration beaded his upper lip. His hand shook as he pulled a handkerchief out of his breast pocket and dabbed at his mouth, then his forehead.

"The tide was out, and the moon full and bright. I'll never forget seeing her in that white cotton dress—so still and—" The mayor's eyes went big and round—his face contorted in pain. He grabbed his stomach. The nearly full plate slithered to the ground, and Mayor Ames crumpled over on top of it.

# 15

One cry of help from Jennie brought Hawk and several others running.

"What happened?"

"I'm not sure. He may have choked on something." Jennie struggled to get the mayor into a sitting position. "He's too heavy for me."

Hawk took over and did a finger sweep of the mayor's mouth, then hoisted him up. Grabbing him around the chest from behind, he made a fist and pulled hard against him, easily executing the Heimlich maneuver Jennie had been attempting.

Hawk's efforts to revive the mayor failed. Jennie ran into the house and called 9–1–1. Thankfully, two of the guests were doctors, and within fifteen minutes the mayor was on his way to the hospital. Hawk and Mrs. Ames followed the ambulance in the limo after asking Gram to take over as host.

Speculations about the mayor's sudden illness ran from food poisoning to gall stones to a heart attack. Whatever had happened seemed to make people extra charitable. Every work of art sold, and people handed Gram checks for $500 to $50,000.

Gram figured the campaign fund against the gambling initiative had raised around half a million dollars. Enough to launch a respectable counterattack.

That was the good news. The bad news was that Mayor Ames would never see the fruits of his efforts. Most of the one hundred or so guests had gone home by the time Sheriff Joe Adams returned to tell them of the mayor's death.

With Ryan and Jennie's help, Annie had loaded up the leftover food and dishes. Now she sat on a white folding chair staring at the one remaining platter on the stained linen table cloth. "It couldn't have been my food. You know how careful I am."

"He was poisoned, Annie." Joe hunkered down in front of her. "Now, I'm sure you had nothing to do with it, but somebody put something in whatever he'd been eating or drinking."

Annie grabbed Joe's hand. "You have to find out who. Something like this could ruin my business. It's all I have."

"We'll do our best. Right now, though, I have to run samples of all the food over to the lab in Lincoln City for the medical examiner. And I need a list of everyone who helped set up and handled the food." He was talking to her as one would a wounded child. Gentle and reassuring. Jennie wondered if maybe they had feelings for each other. Joe let go of Annie's hand and stood.

Annie sighed. "That would be Greg. My regular assistant quit, so Greg helped me set up. I did all the cooking and food handling, though. He wasn't here all that long."

"Greg?" Joe frowned. "A little out of his league, isn't it? Since when did he start catering?"

"He and Todd help sometimes when I'm in a pinch." Annie's gaze traveled from her clasped hands to Joe's face. "I know what you're thinking, but Greg didn't do it. He didn't like the mayor—everyone knows that. I didn't especially care for him either—not after what he did to my father and the way he's treated Todd. But I certainly wouldn't kill him." Her voice rose as she did.

"Okay, calm down." Joe's hands closed over her

shoulders. "It's just that I have to consider every possibility."

"Helen." Joe turned toward Gram. "While I'm dealing with the food, would you see if you can find the guest list? Mrs. Ames says there was one on the mayor's desk."

"You'll need a key," Jennie volunteered.

Joe flashed her an exasperated look. "And just how would you know that?"

"Um—I heard someone talking in there earlier." Jennie repeated the conversation and added, "When I checked the door it was locked. Then the mayor and Senator Baker went in. I was going to eavesdrop, but Hawk stopped me."

"A good thing." Joe frowned. "You should have come to me instead of playing junior detective."

Jennie bristled. "I was going to. I only wanted to find out who they were."

"Right."

Jennie told him about the Native American who'd been talking to Mrs. Ames, and Joe wrote the information down.

"You were with the mayor when he collapsed?" Joe asked.

Jennie nodded, trying to recall the details of what they'd talked about and how he'd acted.

For the next two hours, Joe and his deputies methodically covered every inch of the kitchen and Annie's van. They also moved everyone inside when it started drizzling to question the remaining guests—the three artists and Jennie, Ryan, Gram, and Senator Baker. They were all sitting in the family room like suspects in an Agatha Christie mystery.

The senator railed at Joe. "I can't understand why you're wasting precious time questioning honest folks like us while a killer is running loose out there somewhere."

Joe leaned back in his chair. "The more thoroughly we investigate the crime scene, the better our chances of discovering who did it."

"Then talk to that McGrady girl. She was with him— maybe she knows something."

"You were with him, too, Senator—in his office, not ten minutes before—" Jennie sank back when Joe gave her a keep-quiet sign.

Turning back to Senator Baker, Joe asked, "What were you and the mayor talking about in his office?"

"The campaign. We were planning our strategy for coming out against the gambling initiative. I can assure you I had nothing to do with Forrest's death."

No one did, or at least they wouldn't admit it.

———

Two days later Jennie made a breakfast of blueberry pancakes and bacon. Nick was trying to eat while pretending to read a section of newspaper J.B. had given him. J.B. peered over his paper. "Says here the mayor died from eating toxic mussels found in the cioppino he'd eaten."

"No kidding." Jennie set her piece of pancake back onto her plate. "I ate some of that—it was great. How come it didn't affect me?"

"Good question. Says here Annie had held a portion out just for him. He ate three bowls of it all told."

"Hmm. I had some from the second batch. Maybe the bad mussels were only in the first one. Still, that doesn't explain why no one else got sick."

"No one else was affected?" Gram asked.

"Apparently not." J.B. ducked back behind the paper. "The pathologist says they only found traces of the toxin in the pot."

"What does that mean for Annie?" Gram asked. "They certainly don't still suspect her."

"Not at all." J.B. folded the paper and set it aside. "They found some of the toxin in one of the packages from the processing plant. Which means the supplier may have accidentally gotten some bad shellfish in their stocks. There's a danger of that during the summer months. They're guessing that since it's a naturally occurring toxin that the mayor just got a higher concentration of it than anyone else."

"Does that mean they don't think anyone poisoned him?" The explanation seemed a little too pat.

"That's what it says," J.B. replied. "And I suspect they're right. It would be very difficult to single out the mayor's clams. If someone poisoned the entire batch, anyone could have gotten them. And bivalve shellfish are not generally used as a murder weapon."

"Well, I for one am glad to hear it was accidental." Gram picked up a piece of crisp bacon and waved it as she spoke. "I must say, even one suspicious death in Bay Village is more than enough. And with poor Charlie—Joe still doesn't have any leads on the stabbing. At least Annie's no longer a suspect. She's been beside herself with worry. She already has a full plate with her cousin being blamed for Jessica's death and caring for her father."

"Hey, Papa." Nick lifted J.B.'s paper. "How about reading me the funnies?"

J.B. ruffled Nick's hair. "That's a fine idea. As soon as we finish breakfast we'll take our papers into the living room."

Gram raised an eyebrow at J.B. and smiled. "It might be best if you both set your papers aside and finished your meal."

J.B. winked at Nick. "Your gram's right, lad." They obediently folded the newspapers and concentrated on breakfast.

Something nagged at Jennie, trying to trigger a memory, but it didn't come—maybe later. "Gram? After the benefit when Joe was questioning Annie, she said she didn't like the mayor because of her father. What was that all about?"

"That's something you'll have to ask Annie, I'm afraid. I do know he was injured in a logging accident, but I have no idea how it connects to the mayor."

Jennie finished off her breakfast. The puzzle seemed to

have a lot of non-connecting pieces. She'd already surmised that the mayor's and Jessica's deaths and the attack on Charlie were all somehow tied in to the gambling initiative. In fact, the more she thought about it, the more certain she became. With Todd still in jail, he couldn't have murdered the mayor—or attacked Charlie. That left a killer on the loose—someone who would stop at nothing to get the gambling initiative passed.

Greg remained on her suspect list—especially since he liked to gamble. And he had been on the premises. Hawk definitely went on the list. And Travis—the fired campaign manager. Of course she had to add Senator Baker and the stranger she'd seen at the benefit. Gram seemed to think Annie was innocent, but Jennie wasn't about to eliminate her yet. There were other possibilities as well.

"Jennie?" Gram waved a hand in front of her face. "What are you so deep in thought about?"

"I still think there's a connection to the gambling. Suppose the pro-gambling guys hired a hit man to kill the mayor and hurt Charlie."

"An interesting premise, lass." J.B. leveled a tell-me-more gaze on her.

Jennie went through her list of suspects and ended with Hawk.

"Hawk?" J.B. raised a silver eyebrow and glanced at Helen.

"Yeah," Jennie went on. "The guy is everywhere. He stopped me from going to eavesdrop on the mayor and the senator. He found Charlie—his uncle runs a casino—"

"I don't think that's—"

"No, it's true. You need to meet Hawk, then you'll understand."

"You must stop this line of thinking, lass. It'll get you nowhere."

"J.B.'s right, darling," Gram said. "It's time to let it go."

Jennie folded her arms and sank back into her chair. "That's what Joe said too. But I don't know if I can. I keep thinking about it and—"

"Perhaps you'd better tell her," Gram said. "We can certainly trust her not to say anything, but if she persists she might cause some damage."

In that moment Jennie knew—it didn't take a mind reader to decipher it. She should have seen it sooner. Jennie pictured the tall, lean man—the *chauffeur* who wore a shoulder holster and carried a .38 special like her father's and J.B.'s "You don't have to tell me. Hawk is FBI, isn't he? He's the one Joe said was on the case."

"That's about the size of it." J.B. sounded weary. "He's a good man—one of the best. Thanks to his uncle, he's managed to get himself into a key position."

"His uncle? You mean the casino operator?"

"I can't tell you more than that. Now you need to stay clear and let the man do his job."

Jennie closed her eyes. "I'll try. It's just that things keep happening when I'm there. I can't not think about it."

"Thinking is fine. Just don't act on your suspicions."

Gram's hand closed over Jennie's. "How would you like to go with me today, Jennie? I have a few errands to run, and I'd like to stop and see Mari Ames."

"Sounds good." With Charlie back to work and Ryan working for Greg, Jennie had been wondering what she'd do with herself.

On the way into town, they stopped to see Mari Ames. When they pulled into the driveway next to a black town car, Micky skateboarded toward them, veered off, and hit a makeshift ramp. He and the skateboard went airborne, executed a mid-air somersault, and came down on the board.

Jennie congratulated him on his perfect landing but got no response. His mouth was a thin, flat line on a mannequin-like face.

"Mom's not in the house," Micky finally said when they stepped onto the porch. "She's in her studio—above the garage." He pointed to the exterior steps attached to the two-car garage. "She's been in there since . . . for two days."

Gram glanced at the garage's upper windows, her face a study in compassion. "Has someone been here to care for her—and you?"

"I've been bringing her food, but she won't eat." His lower lip quivered, but only for a moment. Anger replaced the hurt Jennie had seen in his eyes. "I can take care of myself. I don't need her. I don't need anybody." Micky pushed off, rolling toward the ramp again.

Jennie and Gram looked at each other, then headed for the stairway.

# 16

Gram reached the top of the stairs first. The door opened, nearly hitting her.

The Native American Jennie had seen at the benefit backed out. "I'm sorry for your troubles, Mrs. Ames, but I'll expect you to honor your husband's debts." He closed the door and spun around. If Jennie and Gram's presence surprised him, he didn't show it. His dark eyes assessed them. "Excuse me." He squeezed by them on the narrow landing.

Jennie waited until he reached his car, then nudged her grandmother. "That's the guy who was at the benefit."

Taking a pen and pad from her handbag, Gram jotted down the license plate number. "We'll call Joe. First, though, we'd better see to Mari."

Mari Ames sat at a spinning potter's wheel. Gray, wet clay oozed between her fingers as her hands circled a spinning pot. A bowl, Jennie surmised, viewing the stacks of similarly shaped items already thrown and sitting on shelves. Mari glanced up at them as they entered but didn't seem to see them. Her gaze went immediately back to the wet clay. She inserted one hand into the pot and with the other began at the base and worked her way up. The piece grew wider and taller, then slumped in the middle, like rolls of fat on a sumo wrestler.

The potter's shoulders slumped as well. She pinched her

lips together and squeezed the fallen pot between her fingers, then slung a glob of it into a slush bucket. What had begun as a bowl or a cup now sank into the mire—a meaningless lump. Jennie pulled her gaze from the disturbing sight.

Mari looked up at Jennie, her eyes glazed and unfocused. "Jessica. You've come back. I knew you would." A thin smile curved her lips. "You're just in time to help me plan for the party."

Jennie stepped back. Mari Ames had gone over the edge.

Gram moved behind Mari and took hold of her shoulders, speaking in soothing tones. "You need to stop now, Mari. It's time to go inside and rest."

"No!" Mari twisted away. "I have so much to do. Did you see him? That horrible man is spreading rumors about my husband. He told me Forrest and Jessica were dead and that I needed to face facts. He said I had to pay the bill—"

"Jennie." Gram placed her hands on Mari's shoulders again. "Go call Dr. Hanley. His number is in the book. Tell him what's going on and ask him to come over."

Jennie ran out the door and slipped twice on the damp stairs. The house was unlocked, and Mrs. Ames' once spotless kitchen had been thoroughly trashed. At least that's what Jennie thought at first. Then she realized it was just the victim of neglect.

Dirty dishes filled the sink and cluttered every counter. Leftover food sat in pots on the stove. And it smelled like week-old garbage.

Jennie ignored the mess and hurried to the phone. After rummaging through the phone book, she found and dialed Dr. Hanley's number.

"I'll be right there," Dr. Hanley told her when she'd explained that Mrs. Ames was hallucinating. "Don't try to dissuade her. She might stay calmer thinking you are Jessica for now."

As Jennie hung up the phone, she noticed an empty envelope on the counter from the Soaring Eagle Casino. It was addressed to Mayor Ames. Jennie picked it up. Why would the mayor be getting a letter from the casino? A contribution? Not likely. An advertisement? Jennie folded the envelope, stuffed it in her pocket, then hurried back to play Jessica to the very confused Mrs. Ames.

———

Dr. Hanley settled Mari down with a sedative and or-dered her to bed. Jennie offered to stay and care for her and Micky until Mari's sister in Portland could come later that afternoon.

While Mrs. Ames slept, Jennie made a lunch of chicken noodle soup and a peanut butter and jelly sandwich for Micky. While he ate, she started cleaning the kitchen.

"You don't have to do that," Micky said through a mouth-ful of sandwich.

"I know, but I want to."

He swallowed. "We have a cleaning lady. Mrs. Olsen comes in once a week."

"Is she coming today?" Jennie grimaced as she picked up a plate thickly coated with dried orange-colored sauce.

"Nope. Tomorrow."

"I'm not sure this place can last that long. Besides, I still owe you for saving my life. Remember?" Having cleaned out one of the double sinks, Jennie plugged it, ran hot water, squeezed in dish soap, then put the grungiest dishes in to soak.

Jennie pulled out a chair across from Micky. "I'm curious about something."

He shoveled in a spoonful of soup and slurped in a couple of noodles. "Like what?"

"Why didn't you tell someone your mom needed help?"

"She told me not to. 'Sides, I coulda taken care of things."

"Right—like you've been taking care of the kitchen?"

Micky's gaze dropped to his half-eaten sandwich. "I fixed us food. I didn't know what else to do."

Jennie chewed on her lower lip. She was being too hard on him. Losing a sister and father within a matter of weeks had to be devastating. Even if he put on a macho act at times and pretended like he didn't care, Jennie knew he did. "It's okay. I didn't mean to criticize you."

"I guess I should have called somebody—I just didn't know who. Mom seemed okay in some ways. It wasn't till she got that letter—" He stopped as if he'd said too much.

Following a hunch, Jennie pulled the envelope out of her back pocket. "The one from the casino?"

His eyes widened. "She tore it up—how did you. . . ?"

"I don't have the letter, only the envelope. I found it on the kitchen counter." Jennie set the envelope on the table. "Do you know what was in it?"

He shook his head hard enough to jiggle the table. "No, Mom didn't tell me. It must have been bad. She tore it into pieces."

"Micky, this could be really important. It might help us find out what happened to your dad and maybe even your sister. What happened to the letter? Did she throw it away?"

"I . . . I think so. She was standing by the sink tearing it up. She yelled at me to get out, so I did. I've never seen her so mad. Maybe she threw it in the garbage can under the sink. After that she went to her studio and wouldn't come out."

"Well, there's only one thing to do." Jennie took a deep breath to prepare herself for the unpleasant task ahead. She got up and opened the cupboard below the sink. After pulling the white plastic bag free of the sturdy garbage can, Jennie lined the can with a new bag. She opened several drawers.

"What are you looking for?"

"Rubber gloves." The words had just come out when she

found a pair beside a stack of dish towels. Slipping them on, she began transferring trash.

"You're not going to dig through all that garbage, are you? What if it isn't there?"

"I have to look." Jennie couldn't explain what drove her to root through the disgusting mess of papers, cans, and rotting food, but she had to know what had set Mari off.

Jennie spotted a scrap of white paper and held it up and waved it. "I found one."

She rescued at least a dozen pieces of the letter, some wet and slimy from food waste and coffee grounds. Micky watched her for a few minutes, then joined her on the floor, methodically sifting through the mess.

When they'd finished, Jennie set the scraps of paper on the kitchen table, wiped off the worst of the garbage, and patted them dry with a paper towel. "There. Now all we need to do is put them together."

Not an easy task. She discarded all the pieces without writing and assembled only those containing type. As the puzzle came together, Jennie began to understand why Mrs. Ames had reacted so violently. Though stains made it difficult to read, the message was clear.

> Dear Mayor Ames:
>
> We regret to inform you that we can no longer extend credit to you at the casino. Your current debt of $500,000 must be paid immediately or we will be forced to take legal action. It has become apparent that gambling has become an obsession. . . .

"What are you doing?" Mari Ames shrieked. Her hair stood at odd angles. Her wild gaze darted from the table to Jennie. Jennie backed away.

Mrs. Ames swept the table with her arm, scattering the papers all over the floor. "You had no right!" She straightened and pointed to Micky. "Go to your room. I'll deal with you later."

Micky opened his mouth to argue, then shut it. His jaw twitched as he pushed the chair he'd been sitting in to the floor, kicked it away, and left the room. Mari waited until Micky had gone, then turned on Jennie. "I want you out of my house. You had no right to snoop through my trash."

"I thought it would help find out who killed your husband and—"

"I tore that piece of junk up for a reason. That letter was a lie. My husband is against gambling—everyone knows that. Those terrible people are trying to discredit him. It's a conspiracy. They'll stop at nothing to bring gambling into Bay Village. They killed Jessica and now they've killed Forrest." Mari walked to the cupboard near the stove and retrieved a cup, then picked up the teakettle and started to pour a cup of water.

"You need to take the letter to Sheriff Adams. He can verify if it's true or not." The sculpture Jessica had created took on an alarming reality. The Ames family was not at all what they seemed. Jessica's book on gambling addictions. It all made sense now. The mayor had a gambling problem. Had Jessica confronted him? Had he killed his own daughter to protect his dark secrets? How deep was the mayor's deception? Was he really against the gambling initiative like he'd claimed?

And the money stolen from Charlie. Had the mayor stolen campaign funds to pay his debts? But then who had killed the mayor? Too many questions. Jennie needed time to find the answers. She needed to take this new information to Joe. She needed to get away from Mari Ames. "Let's call Joe." Jennie inched toward the phone.

"No." Mari slammed down the teakettle and yanked open a drawer. Pulling out a butcher knife, she raised it over her head and dove toward Jennie.

# 17

Jennie ducked. The knife crashed into the dishes soaking in the sink. Water sloshed over the rim and onto Mari's clothes. She moaned, sounding like a wounded animal, righted herself, then staggered toward Jennie again.

Jennie backed around the table, putting it between them. She let her gaze leave Mari for half a second, trying to orient herself. Jennie had to get to the door, but the table and the crazed woman blocked her way.

Mari raised her arm again, then staggered and fell against the table. The knife clattered to the floor. Mari slumped onto a kitchen chair, folded her arms on the table, and buried her face in her arms. She reminded Jennie of a toy whose batteries had run down.

"What's the use?" Mari rocked back, her arms hung loosely at her side. "I knew I wouldn't be able to hide it forever."

Jennie swallowed hard. She could escape now, but there didn't seem much point. Whatever demon had driven Mari to attack Jennie seemed to have deserted her, leaving her as lifeless as the clay she'd been working with that morning. Jennie kicked the knife into a far corner for safekeeping and reached for the phone. Her gaze fixed on Mari, she dialed 9–1–1. Jennie doubted the woman would try to hurt her again but had no intention of letting down her guard.

After reporting the incident and asking for assistance, Jennie hung up. When Mari didn't make any attempt to move, Jennie went back to the table but didn't sit down. "It's true, isn't it? Your husband owing all that money?"

Mari drew in a deep, shuddering sigh. "Yes. Jessica tried to tell me about his gambling—I didn't believe her."

"That man who was in your studio this morning—is he from one of the casinos?"

Mari nodded. "Soaring Eagle. His Name is Blake Elan."

"He was at the benefit Wednesday night too."

"He came to talk to Forrest and me. I guess he thought I should know about my husband's gambling addiction."

"Why didn't you go to the police?"

"I didn't think it mattered. Forrest was a good mayor. Why ruin his reputation now that he's dead?"

———

When Joe and two other deputies arrived, Jennie explained what she'd found and how Mari had reacted. Dr. Hanley came as well, insisting that Mari be admitted to a psychiatric hospital.

Joe and his crew gathered up the evidence and put Mari in a squad car to transport her to Meadow Brook, a facility located about thirty miles south. Dr. Hanley had called ahead to have her admitted and planned to meet her there.

Jennie gave her statement but decided not to press charges. Mari Ames had enough trouble.

She stayed at the house with Micky until Mari's sister, Chris Nelson, arrived at two.

"Micky," Jennie called. He'd gone upstairs to get a video a few minutes before. "Your aunt is here."

"I sure appreciate your looking after him, Jennie."

"No problem. He's a neat kid. Um . . . have you heard how Mrs. Ames is doing?"

"The doctor said she's quieted down. She's worried

about Micky—that's a good sign. Mick and I will drive down to see her."

"That's good. Tell her . . . tell her I'm thinking about her."

"I will."

Micky dragged down the stairs carrying a Nike bag. "Hi, Aunt Chris." He stepped into her embrace.

"Are you ready to go?"

"I guess."

They locked up the house and headed for the car. Micky looked at Jennie. "Thanks for all you did."

Jennie nodded, not trusting herself to speak. It hurt to see such a great kid going through so much heartache. "Um, listen . . ." She settled an arm across his shoulders and gave him a hug. "Keep in touch, okay?"

"Yeah." He glanced up at his aunt. "Could you stop by Don's place? I gotta tell him good-bye."

"Of course." Chris took the keys to the house from Jennie. "Can I drop you off somewhere?"

"Thanks, but I'll walk. My grandmother lives nearby."

They left then, and Jennie offered up several prayers for her new young friend and his mother while she walked back to Gram's.

Ryan met her in the driveway. "You look beat. What's going on?"

"It's a long story. Let's go down to the rocks, and I'll fill you in."

After leaving a note for Gram and J.B., they took the familiar trail through the woods. Out on the rocks, the sun was shining, and judging from the few puffs of clouds on the horizon, they were in for a gorgeous afternoon. Jennie just wished she could enjoy it more. Her mind seemed lost in heavy gray clouds, and she couldn't see much of anything. Finding out about the mayor's gambling addiction had done nothing except to complicate matters even more. Jennie waited until they were seated, then filled him in on the letter and Mrs. Ames' breakdown.

When she'd finished, Ryan whistled. "Unbelievable. Maybe that's what Jessica was portraying in her clay sculpture. Her dad's addiction and her mom's denial."

"It explains the book I found on gambling addictions too. Jessica had told her mom, but Mrs. Ames said she didn't believe it."

"I'll bet Mrs. Ames knew all along—even before Jessica— and just kept it a secret. In fact, maybe Jessica threatened to tell, so Mari killed her."

Jennie shuddered. "I can't believe she'd do that. Jessica was her daughter."

"It happens. Mari Ames stood to lose everything if word got out that her husband had a gambling addiction."

Jennie hugged her knees and drew in a deep breath of crisp ocean air. "I feel so bad for that family."

"Me too. What's gonna happen to Micky now that his mom's gone?"

"His aunt is taking him back to Portland with her in the morning."

"That's good." Ryan reached for Jennie's hand and wove his fingers through hers. "I talked to Todd today."

"And . . ."

"He apologized for lying to me."

"Good—so are you friends again?"

"Yeah. I just wish we could prove he didn't kill Jessica. He still swears he didn't go back to talk to her that night. And if he's telling the truth, that means Mayor Ames was lying, or someone stole Todd's car, or it was someone with a car like Todd's."

"That's unlikely—there aren't that many powder blue '57 Chevies around."

"True. And after what you told me about Jessica's

parents, I'll bet anything the mayor was lying—maybe to protect his wife."

"And his reputation." Jennie gave Ryan's hand a reassuring squeeze. "Anyway, I wouldn't worry too much about Todd. The mayor's actions will discredit him and cast doubt on his testimony. I have a feeling Todd will be acquitted."

"I hope so." A wide grin lit up his eyes. "Hey, I have a surprise for you."

"What?"

"Tomorrow you and I are going whale watching."

"You're kidding."

"Nope. You know I've been helping Greg out with his business. . . ."

Jenny nodded.

"Well, Greg said I was ready to take a boat out alone. I can't take a tour yet, but he said it would be okay to bring you."

Jennie arched an eyebrow. "Taking a lot for granted, aren't you?"

"What do you mean?"

Jennie's smile crept through despite her determination to keep a straight face. "I mean, what if I don't want to go?" She did, of course. She just didn't want Ryan making plans without asking.

"Oh, I get it." He chuckled and wrapped an arm around her neck and drew her close, forehead to forehead, nose to nose. "Let me rephrase that. How'd you like to go whale watching with me tomorrow?"

Jennie held her breath and closed her eyes, stilling the butterflies in her stomach. "I'd like that very much."

———

When Jennie arrived back at the house, she and Gram drove into Lincoln City where they planned to shop for school clothes and meet J.B. for dinner. Since J.B. had some business in town, they'd asked Ryan to watch Nick.

Gram listened with interest as Jennie filled her in on the letter from the Soaring Eagle Casino and her run-in with Mari.

"I'm not sure I even want to speculate as to who did what. This has turned into a muddy mess, and I'm glad I don't have to clean it up."

"Me too," Jennie said with less conviction than she felt. While she'd have preferred to spend more time talking about possible suspects, Gram clearly didn't.

Gram picked up an envelope from the console beside her and handed it to Jennie.

"I talked to Charlie today, and he said to give you this."

Inside was a thank-you card and a check for $350. "Wow! I didn't expect this much."

"Charlie said he was giving you a bonus for a job well done."

"Great timing," Jennie said, sticking it in her handbag. "I know just how to spend it."

———

By the time they'd finished shopping, over $200 of her check had been spent. At six, they trudged back to the car and stashed shoes, jeans, shirts, underwear, and three new mysteries in the trunk.

Fifteen minutes later they walked into the Kyllos Restaurant at "D" River. J.B. had already been seated, but he wasn't alone. Hawk and Blake Elan were sitting with him. Jennie felt a moment's panic. Was J.B. into gambling too? The panic subsided when she remembered Hawk was FBI.

Once Gram and Jennie had been seated, J.B. made the introductions. Jennie was surprised at J.B.'s openness as he told her Hawk's real name was actually John Elan. John didn't fit him—Hawk did. Jennie thought it odd that Hawk and J.B. *and* Hawk's uncle would be together—unless they'd completed the investigation and Hawk was no longer under cover. Maybe now that the mayor was dead, he didn't need to pretend.

"So how are you, Jennie?" Hawk asked. "Heard about your run-in with Mrs. Ames."

"I'm okay." Even knowing he was an agent didn't calm the uneasiness she felt around him. "Have you heard how she is?"

"Not real great. Looks like she may be doing time."

"For what?"

"Killing her husband."

Jennie nearly choked on her ice water. "You really think Mrs. Ames killed him?"

Gram frowned. "I thought his death was accidental."

"So did we until we found a vial of the concentrated shellfish toxin in Mrs. Ames' closet."

Gram shook out her napkin. "Not something most people have lying around the house, is it?"

"No, it isn't. But a shellfish laboratory up north had reported a break-in last week. A couple of vials of the stuff were missing."

Even though Jennie had narrowly missed being stabbed by the woman, she had a hard time seeing Mari Ames as a cold-blooded killer and said as much. "Maybe the toxin was planted." Everyone's gaze shifted to her. She squirmed under their scrutiny and felt her cheeks grow hot.

Hawk leveled his penetrating dark gaze on her as if to say, *Who do you think you are to have an opinion?*

"Tell us what you're thinking, lass." J.B.'s serious response to her question gave her courage to go on.

"Mrs. Ames was trying to hide the mayor's problem. Murdering him would have called everyone's attention to their family. I mean—why go to all the trouble of hiding it, then commit murder?"

135

"You have a point," Hawk said, "but we weren't supposed to find out."

"Then why would she stash the toxin at her house—and why didn't the police find it before?"

He shrugged. "She's not too rational—you've seen that for yourself. We have an even stronger motive than the gambling. Mrs. Ames blames her husband for Jessica's death. We figured his daughter knew about the gambling and confronted him. Jessica no doubt threatened to go public. He may have felt he needed to silence her."

"Do you have children, Hawk?" Gram asked.

"No, ma'am."

"I thought so. Most parents wouldn't dream of hurting their children. Some do, of course, but to kill a child deliberately . . ." She shook her head. "I can't imagine Mari or Forrest doing that. They adored Jessica."

"That may be, Mrs. Bradley, but Mayor Ames had a lot to lose, and people with addictions don't always make rational decisions."

Jennie's heart hurt. How could one family get so messed up? She focused on her menu, wishing she could forget the entire ordeal. If Hawk was right, it would be over. Todd would be vindicated. Mrs. Ames would be arrested. Unfortunately, it didn't *feel* over.

Hawk paused when the waiter came to take their orders then went on. "Looks like we were right about the gambling initiative, J.B. While Ames was coming out against the gambling initiative publically, privately he had big-time ties in Vegas. Seems he made a deal with a number of casino owners to back his venture. And I do mean *his* venture. He was all set to build the biggest casino on the West Coast."

Blake shook his head. "The man was a phony through and through. If it hadn't been for his gambling addiction, he might have pulled it off."

"Did you determine whether he had any local backers?" J.B. asked.

"I'm still checking out the possibility," Hawk responded. "With the complexity of the case, he must have had at least one person working with him."

"He did," Jennie said. "During the benefit he was in his office talking to someone. I told Joe about it. One guy said something about things being under control. The other guy—I think it must have been the mayor—was worried about Charlie finding out. They must have been planning something because the other guy said there wouldn't be any slip-ups."

Hawk glanced at J.B. "Joe didn't say anything to me about that." His already small eyes turned to narrow slits. "Must have been when Ames sent me to get some papers he'd left in his office at city hall. I was gone fifteen minutes—max."

"Whoever it was," Jennie said, "must have been the one who worked Charlie over and stole the campaign funds."

Blake leaned back when the waiter brought his coffee. "Personally, I think you should check out the sheriff. We had one go bad on us a while back—maybe we have another crook in the bunch. While you're at it you might want to have a crack at Senator Baker. You know what they say about power corrupting."

Jennie thought maybe Hawk should investigate his uncle, too, but didn't say so.

Hawk tossed J.B. an apologetic glance before answering. "With all due respect, uncle, we've investigated both men and there's no reason to suspect them. However, I intend to keep an open mind."

"See that you do, nephew, see that you do." Blake Elan's regal posture and sincere tone nearly erased Jennie's suspicion of him.

By the time their dinners arrived, Jennie felt thoroughly confused. There were too many possible answers to the questions that continued to haunt her, and none of them quite fit. Who killed Jessica? And why? Like Gram, Jennie had a hard time thinking of any parent being bad enough or desperate enough to kill their own child. "I keep trying to make sense of it. I guess I can go along with Mayor Ames killing Jessica to keep her quiet, but I just can't see Mrs. Ames killing her husband."

Gram squeezed Jennie's shoulder. "It is hard to imagine, but we need to remember Mari has suffered a great deal of trauma."

"Not only that, Jennie," Hawk said, "she had means and opportunity. According to Annie Costello, Mrs. Ames oversaw the catering operation and was in and out of the kitchen several times. Annie made two batches of cioppino. The second had no trace of the toxin. Mrs. Ames was there when Annie made the first batch, but not when she made the second."

"Another consideration," Blake added, "is that despite Mrs. Ames' being so upset about the debt, she has plenty of money to cover it."

"I'm afraid they may be right," J.B. added. "Mrs. Ames is a wealthy woman in her own right. She held a million-dollar life insurance policy on her husband. If she discovered he'd been lying and suspected him of killing her daughter, I believe she might consider getting rid of him."

Jennie kept silent for the rest of the meal. Earlier Gram had called the case a muddy mess. So true. *Sometimes*, she reminded herself, *when the waters are too churned up, it helps to leave them alone until they clear*. That's exactly what she would do. Tomorrow she'd forget all about the murders and the gambling initiative and everyone involved and concentrate on whale watching and hanging out with Ryan.

# *18*

Heaven. Pure heaven. Seagulls flew overhead squawking for handouts. Jennie complied by tossing out pieces of bread she'd brought from Gram's. The sun poured down warm and bright. Jennie sat on the bow of the fishing trawler, letting the wind whip through her hair, pulling it free from its braid. Her thoughts drifted back to Dolphin Island off the coast of Florida and the dolphins she'd grown to love. Gram had taken her there for her sixteenth birthday. It seemed so long ago, but it was only a summer away.

Out here on the ocean she was far removed from Jessica Ames and her father. Far away from whoever had murdered them. At least that had been her plan. But thoughts of Jessica buffeted her mind again and again as forcefully as the wind.

"Jennie, look! Off the starboard side!"

"I see them." Jennie tucked her thoughts away and focused on the performance of two gray whales pausing in their southern migration to play. Well, maybe not to play. They would often use the rocks as cleaning posts to rid themselves of barnacles and other sea life that hitched a ride. But it sure looked like play. Whales, like dolphins, seemed to enjoy performing for the people who took the time to watch. The pair breaching not fifty feet from the boat were no exception.

A huge gray whale arched its body as it came up for air. A high stream of water escaped from its blow hole and dissipated. It dove deep, lifting its tail in a wave. His companion followed suit. Just as suddenly as they appeared, they were gone again, leaving no trace of their existence.

"Keep watching. Maybe they'll surface again." Ryan slipped an arm over Jennie's shoulders. "It's great seeing them up this close."

"I love it. Oh . . ." Jennie's heart skidded to a stop when one of the whales rose not ten feet away from them, blew, then rolled, disappearing once more.

"Hold on!" Ryan grabbed for the railing as the boat teetered in the big mammal's wake. "Whoa. That guy has to be at least fifty feet long."

Jennie vacillated between admiration and fear. If the whales got too careless they could turn their boat into driftwood. "I didn't know they'd come this close."

"Awesome, huh?" Ryan shouted to be heard over the engines. He needn't have bothered. The engines sputtered and died.

Back at the helm, Ryan twisted the key. The motor made a sick attempt to start.

"Maybe you're out of fuel," Jennie suggested.

"I'm not out of fuel. I filled up before we came out." Ryan tried the key again—nothing.

"The fuel gauge is on empty."

Ryan's chilly blue gaze met hers. "I am not out of fuel. It probably registers empty when the engine is off."

"Okay, no need to get huffy. I'm just trying to help."

"Well, don't, okay? Just go sit somewhere. I'll figure it out."

Jennie bit into her lower lip, advising herself to keep her mouth shut. He'd figure it out eventually.

Leaving Ryan to mutter to himself, Jennie went downstairs to the galley to get a drink and something to snack on. She rummaged through the small refrigerator Ryan said he'd stocked the day before. She found a couple cans of soda, a chunk of furry gray-green cheese, and a couple of unmarked plastic containers of who knew what. "Give me a break, Johnson," she muttered. "If this is your idea of—"

Jennie's grumbling turned into a high-pitched yelp when the boat pitched and threw her to the floor. The contents of the refrigerator tumbled out on top of her. One of the soda cans split as it hit the floor, spraying its foamy contents into her face. After trying unsuccessfully to plug the leak, Jennie scrambled to her feet and tossed the can into the sink, then grabbed a towel and began mopping it up.

So much for a fun, relaxing day with Ryan.

She put the other two cans back on the shelf and was wiping root beer off one of the containers when she heard another boat approach. Ryan must have radioed for help. Maybe the Coast Guard or another whale watcher.

Well, good. At least they'd be rescued. Not that she'd been all that worried. She wasn't in too much of a hurry to go topside. Ryan wouldn't appreciate her assistance anyway. Apparently he felt taking care of downed vessels was a guy thing.

She wiped off the opaque white plastic container and froze. The message had been facing away from her earlier. There was no fancy scientific name, no professional label. Someone had drawn a crude skull and crossbones beneath the words, *bivalve shellfish toxin*.

Jennie pushed the container back into the fridge, trying to make some sense of its presence. Who had put it there and why? Greg? Annie? Both had access to the boat. Or maybe it was another case of planted evidence. This was Greg's boat. He'd been at the benefit helping Annie. One way or another she had to let the authorities know about the toxin.

She latched the fridge and hurried up the stairs, finding Ryan at the bridge, steering. The engines were still dead. The boat she'd heard was pulling away. "What's going on?" Jennie put her hand on his shoulder.

"Greg's giving us a tow." He glanced at her, his face just short of crimson. "There's a leak in one of the fuel lines."

Jennie watched the cable between the two boats grow taut. She didn't like the idea of Greg towing them, but there wasn't much she could do about it now. She sighed and gave Ryan's shoulder a squeeze. "I'm not sure how to tell you this, but something really strange is going on." She explained what she'd found in the galley.

Ryan frowned. His Adam's apple shifted up and down. "I messed up, Jennie. I was supposed to take the *Lucy S*, not the *Linda Sue*. They look so much alike I just grabbed the first one."

"That explains the lack of food in the galley." Jennie climbed into the passenger seat. "So you want to venture a guess as to why a container of the toxin is on Greg's boat?"

"I don't have a clue. You're the detective. You tell me."

"Maybe Greg is the killer. Maybe he took Todd's car that night and went to talk to Jessica. He was at the benefit helping Annie. He could have been the guy in the mayor's office."

"That would mean he was working for the mayor. Greg wouldn't do that. Besides, why would he kill him? Or Jessica?"

"I don't know. Revenge. To get back at Mayor Ames for what happened to his dad."

Ryan shook his head. "His dad died in a logging accident. Ames owned the company. You don't kill a guy for that."

So that was the connection. "What about Annie? She blamed Mayor Ames for the accident too."

"No way. After all this time? It's like someone is deliberately trying to manufacture evidence on everybody involved. First Todd, then Mrs. Ames. Maybe this whole thing with Mayor Ames was made up too. Maybe he really didn't have a problem with gambling."

"Now that makes no sense at all." Jennie fixed her gaze on the boat towing them. They were picking up speed now and would soon be in Bay Village. She'd get off the boat, thank Greg for the tow, pretend she hadn't found anything, then walk straight to the sheriff's office.

A thread of fear wove itself around Jennie's heart. Something wasn't right. Glancing at her watch, then at the sun behind them, Jennie grabbed Ryan's arm. "What time do you have?"

"Ten. Why?"

"That's what I've got."

"Why all this interest in time? You have an appointment or something?"

"No." Her response came in a pant. "The sun is behind us."

"So?"

"Ryan, don't you see? If we were being towed *in*, the sun would be in *front* of us. Greg is pulling us farther out to sea."

Ryan dragged his hands down his face. "Okay. Let's not panic. There's got to be a reason."

"Right. He's going to kill us."

"No. He wouldn't do that. He's a friend, Jennie."

"You took the wrong boat. Maybe he thinks we saw the toxin. He came on board while I was in the galley, didn't he?"

Ryan closed his eyes and leaned forward, thumping his forehead on the wheel. "Yeah. He wanted to know where you were. When I told him, he got even madder. Told me to hook up the cable so he could tow us in."

"He did it. He killed Mayor Ames."

"Okay, maybe you're right about that too. But it'll be okay. We'll make it. I'll radio for help." While Ryan radioed, Jennie watched Greg lean over something on the back of his boat.

After several tries, Ryan slammed his hand on the console. "The radio's dead. Greg must have disconnected the wires while I was attaching the tow line. Oh, Jen, I'm so sorry."

Jennie slipped off her chair and stepped into Ryan's arms. "Don't give up. We'll make it."

They pitched forward as the boat slowed. "Look!" Ryan grabbed the console to steady himself. "He's lost the tow line. We're drifting again."

"This is bizarre."

Greg had turned around and was coming toward them.

Ryan breathed a deep sigh and hugged her. "It's okay. Maybe the line broke. He's not deserting us."

"He was pulling us out to sea."

"Jennie, relax, will you? I'm sure he has a good explanation."

Greg pulled up alongside the disabled craft and jumped aboard.

"What happened?" Ryan asked. "Why were we headed out?"

"You don't want to know." Greg, knees bent for balance, reminded Jennie of a gorilla. He reached in the pocket of his vest and pulled out a gun.

*When confronted with danger, yell for help and run.* That's what the self-defense manuals say. Unfortunately, Jennie had nowhere to run. And the only people who would hear her screams would be Ryan and the man holding the gun. *So now what? Okay, McGrady,* she told herself. *Just stay calm and look for a way out.*

"W-what are you going to do to us?" Ryan stammered.

"Believe me, Ryan, I wish I didn't have to hurt you. If you'd taken the *Lucy S* . . ." His gaze swept to Jennie. "You found it, didn't you?"

Jennie didn't answer him. "Killing us would be a big mistake, Greg. Since we went out on your boat, the sheriff will be able to tie you to our deaths."

"Don't count on it. All the authorities will know is that you took the wrong boat. This one needed repairs and had a leak in the fuel line. Unfortunately, it blew up with you two on board."

Jennie gulped back the rising panic. She had to stay calm.

"Why did you kill the mayor?" Maybe if she could keep him talking.

"It's a long story."

"So tell it," Ryan insisted. "If you're going to kill us, at least tell us why."

Greg smirked. "Forrest Ames killed my father."

"I thought that was an accident."

"It didn't have to happen. Over and over the men pleaded with Ames to get new equipment, but he wouldn't spend a dime more than he had to. Used all the money to build his big fancy house and get himself set for when the business failed. The scum deserved to die."

Jennie remembered Greg's comment about people paying for their sins. "What about Jessica? Did she deserve to die too?"

He released a jagged sigh. "Yeah. As a matter of fact she did. She broke Todd's heart. He almost killed himself because of her."

"What are you talking about?" Ryan took another step toward him.

Greg waved the gun at them, warning them to stay put. "That night he came home. I heard him drive up, but when he didn't come in, I went out to the garage. He was sitting in his car with the motor running—crying. Todd hadn't cried since our dad died. I took him in and made sure he was okay, then drove over to talk to Jessica. The ring Todd had given her was on the seat. I wanted to shove it down her throat."

Revenge. Jennie pressed back against Ryan. "I can understand why you'd be upset, but—"

"No! No you can't. I'm sick of people saying they understand. You can't possibly know what it's like to—" Greg's dark eyes turned to pebbles. "You're trying to upset me. Get me to make a mistake. That's not going to happen."

Ryan stepped in front of Jennie. "You're right, Greg. I don't understand how you could kill Jessica in cold blood and let your brother go to jail for it."

Greg shook his head. "He'll get off. I hired a good criminal lawyer."

"With what? You said yourself business was bad."

"Let's just say I got all the money I need, thanks to Mayor Ames. He hired me to steal the funds from Charlie and rough him up a bit."

"Rough him up?" Jennie glared at him. "You nearly killed him."

"Yeah—why not? He was set to put Todd away. Now shut up and give me your life jackets."

"Why?" Jennie managed to talk past the lump in her throat.

"Why do you think?"

This was it. They really were going to die. Being this far out without a life jacket, they'd never make it. Maybe there were more on board, she reminded herself. If they had enough time she could get to them. *Oh, God, please help us.* Jennie and Ryan removed the orange jackets and tossed them on the floor in front of Greg. Greg scooped them up, then climbed back on board the other craft. Seconds later he pulled away. Jennie ran toward the back of the boat to the wooden box where life jackets were usually stored. She heard the gunshot about the same time a bullet tore into the deck in front of her.

Ryan grabbed her around the waist and dragged her back. "What are you trying to do, get yourself killed?"

She struggled against him. "Let me go. If I don't get the life jackets, we'll die anyway."

A gunshot rang out again, this time hitting the back of the boat.

"He's trying to blow us up!" Ryan let her go. "We don't have a chance."

"Yes we do. We can jump clear of the boat." Jennie clambered to the starboard side and grabbed the railing. "Who knows how many shots it'll take to—"

Greg fired again. A split second later an explosion ripped the boat apart.

# 19

The force of the explosion threw Jennie into the air. As though caught up in a slow-motion scene, she flew some twenty feet, then sliced into the water. Within seconds the bone-chilling cold and the lack of oxygen shocked her into action. Jennie kicked and crawled upward, gasping as she surfaced.

Something dragged her back. Treading water, she kicked off her shoes, then pulled off her heavy sweat shirt to make herself more buoyant. Otherwise swimming or even treading water would tire her out too quickly.

Jennie glanced around. Panic threatened to pull her under again. High swells lifted her up, then down, making it almost impossible to see anything but water. When the water lifted her, she caught sight of Greg's trawler heading out to sea. He hadn't stuck around to make sure they were dead. But then why would he? The boat had been blown to pieces, and they were too far off shore to swim.

She spent the next precious minutes pleading with God and looking for Ryan, swimming in a circle—or what she thought was a circle, but could find no trace of him in the debris floating around her. She was tiring. Jennie looked for a flotation device—a life jacket or board—anything that would hold her. She could tread water for another fifteen minutes—maybe. But the water was cold, and she could already feel her body temperature dropping. Jennie thought she spotted a life jacket in the distance, but by the time she could get to the spot she thought she'd seen it, it had disappeared.

Several minutes passed before Jennie found a piece of wood big enough to hold her. She hoisted herself on it. Pink salt water dripped onto the white plank. It was then she felt the sting of salt on her cheek and noticed a cut on her hand.

Gathering up her T-shirt, Jennie wrung out the water and pressed it to the wound on her cheek. The board she'd managed to secure was about the size of a surf board—maybe wider. She lay flat on her stomach and continued to paddle around the debris, hoping, praying Ryan had made it out alive.

Half an hour later her arms ached from paddling. Her head hurt. Jennie didn't want to give up, but her body refused to cooperate. She didn't want to think of Ryan drowning so she tried not to think at all. Jennie drew her arms out of the water and rested her head on them. The sun had nearly dried her shirt and pants and taken the edge off the cold.

————

Sometime later Jennie awakened to the sounds of seagulls cawing and the flapping of wings. One gull, then two, landed on her back and pecked at her head.

"Ouch!" She covered her head with one arm and waved them off with the other. Her narrow bed shifted, spilling her into the water. She mounted the board again and tried to orient herself. According to her watch it was noon. The sun would be straight up. "Okay, God, which way do I go?" Jennie scanned the horizon as best she could. She spotted a boat in the distance and started to wave.

"You're losing it, McGrady. A lot of good waving will do. No way they can see you from that distance." She couldn't tell which direction the boat was headed. And she didn't know if she'd be moving toward shore or out to sea. Since it was the only option available at the moment, Jennie dipped in one arm, then the other, and headed toward the vessel.

She didn't make it. The boat soon disappeared. Her feet and forearms had grown numb, her lips parched and dry. The sun had come out again, renewing her hopes, then crushing them again when she realized how low in the sky it hung. It would set soon, leaving her exposed and vulnerable.

*Don't give up. Keep moving. Come on, you can make it.*

"I can't," Jennie argued with the almost audible voice. "I'm too tired, and I don't know which way to go."

*The sun will guide you.*

Jennie lifted her head expecting to see an angel or that bright light she'd heard about from people with near-death experiences. She did see light—a blinding light on the horizon. *The sun.* Jennie could almost feel the adrenalin pump through her veins at the thought. Spinning herself around, Jennie kept the sun behind her and headed toward the shore. She would make it home or die trying.

————

In the distance Jennie heard a strange thumping sound. A boat? Maybe. At the moment, she was too exhausted to care. She tried to loosen her grip on the board so she could brush her hair from her face. Her fingers wouldn't move. She had no idea how far she'd come, only that she had no strength left. When the swells moved her just right, she thought she could see the shoreline and a light or two flickering in the distance. Jennie opened her eyes, then closed them again.

The sound grew louder. A powerful wind buffeted her around and sent her already precarious craft to spinning. Jennie felt the board slip away from her. "No, don't. I'll drown. I . . ."

"Hey, take it easy," someone shouted. "I've got you."

Arms and legs flailing, Jennie struggled to free herself

from whoever was holding her. *Holding her?* Jennie's eyes flew open. A man in a neon orange survival suit was hanging from a cable attached to a Coast Guard helicopter. Another had grabbed her from behind and had a vise grip around her waist.

Jennie stopped struggling. "Where . . . when?"

"Don't try to talk. Just work with us, and we'll have you out of here in no time. I'm hooking a belt around your chest." Then he attached her to the cable and passed her on to his partner. Jennie sent a dozen silent thank-yous to God and to her rescuers on the way up.

Minutes later, wrapped in blankets and drinking hot cocoa, Jennie sat in the helicopter telling her rescuers about Greg Kopelund and his attempt to murder her and Ryan. "Please tell me you found Ryan. I looked for a long time, but . . ."

The guy who'd hauled her out of the water shook his head. No, they hadn't found Ryan and were getting ready to go in when the pilot spotted her.

"We need to keep looking. If I made it, maybe he did too."

"We'll go out again tomorrow at daybreak." The message written on their faces offered little hope.

"How did you know to look for us?"

"Got a call from your grandmother saying you hadn't come in. The boat was still out, and when we couldn't get a radio response we headed out. Been looking for you since around three."

The Coast Guard chopper landed at the base where an ambulance waited to transport her to the hospital. Gram was there when she arrived. Once settled in the emergency room, Jennie sat up on the stretcher.

"Oh, Gram—it was awful . . . and Ryan . . ." The words caught in her throat.

"There, there." Gram wrapped Jennie in her arms and patted her back. "Don't try to talk, just rest. Joe called before you came in to tell us he'd picked up Greg. He'll be by later to get your statement."

After being warmed, poked, and prodded, the ER doctor stitched up the gash on Jennie's jaw and sent her home. She felt numb—like somebody else was occupying her body—moving and talking while she watched from a distance, trying to make some sense of it all.

J.B. had driven to his office in Portland earlier in the day and would be flying to Las Vegas with Hawk to round up the mayor's backers and put an end to the casino sham. Hopefully it would put an end to the gambling initiative as well.

She spent what was left of the day in a fog—sitting mindlessly in front of the TV with Nick, watching Nick play catch with Bernie, and finally at eight-thirty putting Nick to bed.

Exhausted, but too upset to sleep, Jennie stumbled downstairs and joined Gram in the kitchen.

"I made you some chicken noodle soup," Gram said. "When you're done with that I suggest you go to bed."

Jennie shook her head. "How can I sleep knowing Ryan's out there somewhere? I should see how his parents are doing."

"You need to eat . . . and rest." Gram wrapped an arm around Jennie's shoulder.

"What about Joe? He'll need my statement."

"He can see you tomorrow."

"I'll never be able to sleep. Not with Ryan missing."

"You will."

After Jennie had eaten, Gram escorted her up the stairs. Dutifully, Jennie crawled into bed.

Treating her like she might a small child, Gram tucked her in. "Would you like me to pray with you?"

Jennie nodded, then blinked back a landslide of tears while Gram thanked God for bringing Jennie home safely, then asked Him to bring Ryan home as well.

"Gram." Jennie grasped her grandmother's hand. "Do you think he'll make it?"

Gram pressed her lips together. "I honestly don't know, darling. Miracles can happen. After all, they found you."

Jennie tried to sleep but after an hour of tossing gave up. Over and over the explosion rocked her. Thoughts of Ryan injured and drowning and calling for help haunted her. Finally, Jennie got up, wrapped an afghan around her shoulders, and went to the window. The moon was full and bright, cutting a swath of white across the black sea.

"Ryan Johnson," she whispered, looking out at the horizon, "you'd better not die out there. I'll never forgive you. . . ." The tears came again, and this time Jennie didn't try to stop them. There was nothing she could do now except pray and wait.

---

The next morning Joe stopped by as they were finishing breakfast. "How are you doing, Jennie?" A dark shadow lined his jaw.

"Better. Thanks." Even though every muscle in her body hurt, she did feel better. She'd managed to convince herself that Ryan had survived and that the Coast Guard would find him.

"Would you like something to eat?" Gram set a plate of muffins on the table next to a pitcher of orange juice.

"Thought you'd never ask." Joe settled into the chair next to Jennie. "You up to telling me what happened?"

She nodded and gave him a detailed sketch of Greg's confession. "He must have really hated Mayor Ames."

"Revenge runs deep in some folks, Jennie. All that hate was bound to come out sooner or later."

"I still don't understand how it all fits together." Gram set her teacup on the table and sat down.

Joe smeared butter on his muffin. "It gets kind of complicated. Apparently it all boils down to revenge. Greg blamed Mayor Ames for his father's death and never got over it. When Jessica broke up with Todd, the anger flared up again. He went to see Jessica and apparently fought with her."

"It still seems odd that he'd let Todd take the blame."

"I don't think Greg ever meant for Todd to be convicted. More than likely he was playing out all his cards first. Somehow, maybe from Todd or Jessica, Greg found out about the mayor's gambling and started blackmailing him. He apparently planned to get as much money as possible out of the deal, then kill the mayor off."

"Why would Forrest go along with Greg?" Gram asked. "It seems a rather unlikely alliance."

"The mayor probably thought it was better to have Greg working *for* him rather than against him. I have a hunch he was ready to do anything to protect his name at that point. By the way, Jennie," Joe added, "it was Greg you heard in the mayor's office the night of the benefit. Annie told me today she'd seen Greg go in."

"Why didn't she say something earlier?" Jennie stood and began gathering dishes.

"Didn't think it mattered." The sad look in Joe's eyes showed disappointment.

"You think she might be involved too?"

Joe's head came up. "No. Not at all. She volunteered the information as soon as she heard we'd arrested him. She's pretty upset about the whole thing. Still can't believe Greg's capable of murder."

"I guess I can understand that," Gram said. "It's difficult to believe a family member could be involved in any crime—let alone murder."

They talked more about the case—at least Gram and Joe did. Jennie's mind traveled back to the ocean and the rescue efforts. *Please let them find Ryan, God. Please. I don't want him to die.*

# 20

"He's alive," Jennie reassured herself as well as Ryan's mother. Gram and Jennie had gone over to the Johnson house to offer comfort, coffee, and chocolate chip cookies. "He knows survival skills, and he knows the ocean."

Mrs. Johnson sipped at the amaretto-flavored coffee Gram had made. "I keep telling myself that. But we have to face facts. Every minute that goes by lessens his chances." She gave Jennie a vacant look.

Jennie pinched her lips together. She'd break down and cry again if she sat there much longer.

Gram touched Jennie's hand and as if reading her mind said, "You look like you could use some fresh air. Why don't we all take a walk?"

After rounding up Nick and Bernie, the five of them hiked over to Fogarty Creek State Park and wandered along the beach. Jennie jogged ahead with Nick and Bernie. Gram did much better at comforting people than Jennie did. And Mrs. Johnson needed a lot of comforting. What Jennie needed was to find Ryan. Up the beach she noticed a large form. A body? She left Nick to draw pictures in the sand and ran on ahead.

*No, don't even think it, McGrady. It's just a clump of seaweed. It has to be.* But it wasn't seaweed. It was a dead seal.

"Oh . . ." Jennie covered her eyes and ran, dropping to her knees a short distance away. "It isn't fair, God. It just isn't fair. Why Ryan? Why couldn't you have taken me instead?"

After a few seconds, Jennie scrambled to her feet again and ran back to the others. The last thing Mrs. Johnson needed to do was see that poor seal. Jennie told them she wasn't feeling well and insisted on going back to the house.

It was three-thirty by the time they got back. A familiar white Toyota sat in the driveway. Camilla was leaning against it, watching them. Jennie groaned inwardly. Camilla was the last person Jennie wanted to see.

"Hi." Camilla pushed away from the car and walked toward them. When she got closer, Jennie could see she'd been crying.

"I need to talk to you, Jennie."

Gram said she'd be upstairs taking a nap with Nick and left the two girls who loved Ryan Johnson alone. When Jennie drew closer she felt a sting of guilt. Camilla's eyes were as red and puffy as her own. Jennie sighed. "Come on inside."

"Actually, I was hoping you'd have a Coke with me in town. I . . . there's something I need to show you and . . . well, the truth is, I don't want to be here so close to where Ryan lives—lived."

"You had it right the first time. It's too soon to give up hope."

Camilla bit into her lower lip and nodded. "So will you come with me?"

"I guess." Jennie folded her long frame into the Toyota, and within a few minutes they were sitting at Charlie's place ordering drinks. Charlie chatted with them for a while about Greg, then excused himself to wait on customers.

"What did you want to talk to me about?" Jennie puzzled over Camilla's clandestine behavior. After all, the mystery was solved. And this was not the time to argue about who should claim Ryan as a boyfriend.

Camilla reached into her handbag and retrieved some

papers. "I wanted to show you these."

Jennie recognized them immediately. The pages from Jessica's diary. "Where did you get those?"

"I took them. I knew where she kept it and . . ." She looked away. "I shouldn't have done it, but when they arrested Todd I had to do something. I knew he'd never hurt Jessica. I thought she might have written something that would prove he didn't kill her."

Jennie scanned the notes. "Only it implicates him."

*I broke up with Todd tonight,* Jessica had written. *I know he hates me, but it's better this way.*

*Now comes the hard part—talking to Dad. I hope he'll listen to me. Mom says I shouldn't say anything.*

*Sometimes I think it would be better if I could just end it. Here and now. It would be so easy.*

Jessica used the rest of the page to write about what she might do and how she felt about her father's betrayal. Then on the next page wrote

*I can't believe he'd do something like this. I'm going to talk to him tonight. It's late—almost midnight—but I need to know the truth . . . I hear a car . . . Oh no, he's back.*

"I knew it would look bad for Todd," Camilla said.

"So you kept this and told everyone you thought she might have committed suicide."

"She was despondent. She'd been depressed for a long time."

"Well, now we know why. She knew about her father's gambling." Jennie folded the papers and handed them back.

"I think she was planning to commit suicide and that's why she broke up with Todd."

"Could be. But we'll never know that for sure."

"I suppose not." Camilla tucked the pages away. "I guess I should take these to the sheriff."

"That would be wise." Jennie took a sip of her Coke. "You heard about Greg?"

Camilla nodded. "Todd is devastated. He was afraid Greg might have killed her when the mayor insisted he'd seen Todd's car. He convinced himself that Mayor Ames was lying and trying to pin the blame on him. But when he saw the ring, he knew Greg had done it. Greg was the only one who could have taken the ring from Todd's car."

"No wonder things were so confusing. Todd lied over and over—first to protect himself, then to protect his brother."

"The poor guy," Camilla said. "Now he's bearing the guilt of Ryan's . . ."

*Death.*

Jennie pushed her drink aside. "I really don't want to talk about it."

"Sure. Do you want to go back to your grandmother's?"

"No," she snapped. Jennie needed to get away.

Camilla's eyes had turned as gray as the sky and were threatening to rain.

"I . . . I'm sorry." Jennie stared at the table, then brought her gaze back to Camilla. "I shouldn't be getting mad at you. I was thinking about going for a walk. You can go along if you want."

"I'd like that."

They drove back to Gram's, where Camilla parked her car. Jennie led the way to the rocks, not stopping until she reached their cave. "Ryan and I used to come here all the time." She let her gaze drift over the churning water.

Camilla sat on the ledge, hugging her knees. "He really liked you, Jennie. He told me you were the nicest girl he's ever known—and the smartest too."

"I'll bet that made you feel good."

"It was okay. I like Ryan a lot. I probably always will. He's not only great looking, but he's, you know—kind."

"I know." Jennie closed her eyes, remembering their times together. She and Ryan had spent a lot of afternoons and evenings there, watching sunsets and moons and stars and solving the world's problems.

"It's beautiful out here," Camilla said.

Jennie opened her eyes. "Yeah. There's a cove down below—where we go to hunt for agates." Jennie didn't know why, but it suddenly seemed important to be there. "Want to see it?"

"Sure."

Even before she stepped onto the sand Jennie knew why she'd been compelled to come. Her heart slammed into overdrive. A body had been washed ashore, and this was no seal.

"Jennie, look! It's—"

"Ryan!" Jennie raced toward him, stopping just short of where he lay. So still and white. Forcing her feet to move, Jennie took a step closer and knelt beside him. She had to know. Placing a hand on his shoulder, she turned him over.

"Is he. . . ?"

Jennie felt for a pulse. "He's still alive."

"Thank God." Camilla rested a hand on Jennie's shoulder. "What can I do?"

"Go for help. I'll stay with him." Jennie took off her jacket and draped it over him, tucking it around his shoulders. She cradled his head in her lap, talking to him, urging him to hold on.

He opened his eyes once and tried to smile. "You came," he whispered.

"Shh. Of course I came."

---

It took less than an hour for the Coast Guard to rescue Ryan and airlift him to the hospital. Jennie refused to leave his side until he was safely resting on a stretcher in a cubicle in the emergency room and under a doctor's care.

The next morning Jennie rose early and hurried back to the hospital. She'd stayed until ten the night before and at Gram's insistence had gone home to sleep. Now with the light of morning, Jennie needed to make sure Ryan's rescue hadn't been a dream. His being alive was a miracle in more ways than one, and she could hardly believe it. Jennie parked in the nearly empty lot and jogged inside. She paused at the door to Ryan's room. Apparently she wasn't the only one interested in Ryan's miraculous rescue.

"I'm not kidding." Ryan's smile brightened the room—or so it seemed to Jennie. Of course the light could have come from the flashbulbs and television cameras. Ryan was being interviewed by all the major television news teams.

"You're telling us a whale brought you in?" The question came from a man holding a Channel 8 microphone.

"I know it sounds crazy, but it happened. I'd been blown free of the boat and was trying to get to the surface. I must have gotten disoriented and gone down instead of up. Anyway, I felt something huge brush past me. I was panicking by then. All of a sudden this whale came back under me and lifted me clean out of the water."

"And it brought you in to shore?"

"Close enough for me to swim. I made it to the cove but couldn't go any farther. Guess I must have broken my leg in the blast. I wasn't about to give up, though. I knew that sooner or later my girlfriend would come out to the rocks and find me. I just didn't think it would take her so long." Ryan reached for Jennie's hand.

Then the cameras focused on Jennie, who for the umpteenth time told her side of the story.